Brida

Paulo Coelho

Brida

Translated from the Portuguese by
Margaret Jull Costa

HarperCollinsPublishers

Paulo Coelho's website address is **www.paulocoelho.com**

HarperCollins*Publishers*

First published in English in 2008
by HarperCollins*Publishers*
First published in Australia in 2008
by HarperCollins*Publishers* Australia Pty Limited
ABN 36 009 913 517
www.harpercollins.com.au

This edition published by arrangement with Sant Jordi Asociados,
Barcelona, Spain. All rights reserved.

HarperCollins*Publishers*
25 Ryde Road, Pymble, Sydney, NSW 2073, Australia
31 View Road, Glenfield, Auckland 10, New Zealand
1–A, Hamilton House, Connaught Place, New Delhi – 110 001, India
77–85 Fulham Palace Road, London, W6 8JB, United Kingdom
2 Bloor Street East, 20th floor, Toronto, Ontario M4W 1A8, Canada
10 East 53rd Street, New York NY 10022, USA

ISBN 978 0 7322 8741 2

Cover photograph © Mary Taglienti/Getty Images
Typeset in 10.5 on 15pt Sabon by Kirby Jones
Printed and bound in Australia by Griffin Press
70gsm Bulky Book Ivory used by HarperCollins*Publishers* is a natural,
recyclable product made from wood grown in sustainable forests.
The manufacturing processes conform to the environmental regulations
in the country of origin, Finland.

6 5 4 3 2 1   08 09 10 11

... what woman having ten silver coins,
if she loses one of them,
does not light a lamp, sweep the house,
and search carefully until she finds it?
When she has found it, she calls together
her friends and neighbours, saying,
'Rejoice with me, for I have found the coin
that I had lost.'

Luke 15:8–9

For N.D.L. who made the miracles happen,
for Christina, who is one of those miracles,
and for Brida

Brida

Warning

In my book *The Diary of a Magus*, I replaced two of the practices of RAM with exercises in perception learned in the days when I worked in drama. Although the results were, strictly speaking, the same, I received a severe reprimand from my Teacher. 'There may well be quicker or easier methods – that doesn't matter; what matters is that the Tradition remains unchanged,' he said.

For this reason, the few rituals described in *Brida* are the same as those practised over the centuries by the Tradition of the Moon – a specific tradition that requires experience and practice. Practising such rituals without guidance is dangerous, inadvisable, unnecessary and can greatly hinder the Spiritual Search.

Paulo Coelho

Prologue

We used to sit until late at night in a café in Lourdes. I was a pilgrim on the sacred Road of Rome and still had many more days to travel in search of my Gift. She was Brida O'Fern and was in charge of a certain stretch of that Road.

On one such night, I asked if she remembered having felt especially moved when she arrived at a particular abbey that forms part of the star-shaped trail followed by Initiates in the Pyrenees.

'I've never been there,' she replied.

I was surprised. She did, after all, have a Gift.

'All roads lead to Rome,' said Brida, using an old proverb to tell me that Gifts could be awoken anywhere. 'I walked my Road to Rome in Ireland.'

During our subsequent meetings, she told me the story of her search. When she finished, I asked if, one day, I could write it down.

She agreed initially, but whenever we met after that, she kept raising obstacles. She asked me to change the names of those

3

involved; she wanted to know what kind of people would read the book and how they would be likely to react.

'I've no idea,' I said. 'But I don't think that's why you're creating all these problems.'

'You're right,' she said. 'It's because it seems to me such a personal story, and I'm not sure anyone else would get much out of it.'

*   *   *

That's a risk we're now going to take together, Brida. An anonymous text from the Tradition says that, in life, each person can take one of two attitudes: to build or to plant. The builders might take years over their tasks, but one day, they finish what they're doing. Then they find they're hemmed in by their own walls. Life loses its meaning when the building stops.

Then there are those who plant. They endure storms and all the many vicissitudes of the seasons, and they rarely rest. But, unlike a building, a garden never stops growing. And while it requires the gardener's constant attention, it also allows life for the gardener to be a great adventure.

Gardeners always recognise each other, because they know that in the history of each plant lies the growth of the whole World.

The Author

Ireland

Angust 1983–March 1984

Summer and Autumn

want to learn about magic,' said the girl. The Magus looked at her. Faded jeans, T-shirt, the challenging look adopted by all shy people precisely when it's least needed. 'I must be twice her age,' he thought. And despite this, he knew that he had met his Soulmate.

'My name's Brida,' she went on. 'Forgive me for not introducing myself. I've waited a long time for this moment and I'm more nervous than I thought I would be.'

'Why do you want to learn about magic?' he asked.

'So that I can find answers to some of the questions I have regarding life, so that I can learn about the occult powers, and, possibly, how to travel back into the past and forwards into the future.'

It wasn't the first time someone had come to the forest to ask him this. There was a time when he'd been a Teacher who was known and respected by the Tradition. He'd taken on several pupils and believed that the world would change if he could change those around him. But he had made a mistake. And Teachers of the Tradition cannot make mistakes.

'Don't you think you're rather young?'

'I'm twenty-one,' said Brida. 'If I wanted to start learning ballet, I'd be considered too old.'

The Magus made a sign for her to follow him. They set off together through the forest, in silence. 'She's pretty,' he was thinking as the shadows cast by the trees rapidly lengthened and shifted as the sun sank lower on the horizon. 'But I'm twice her age.' This, he knew, meant that he might well suffer.

Brida felt irritated by the silence of the man walking beside her; he hadn't even deigned to respond to her last remark. The forest floor was wet and covered in fallen leaves; she, too, noticed the shadows changing and the rapid approach of night. It would be dark soon and they didn't have a torch with them.

'I have to trust him,' she told herself. 'If I believe that he can teach me magic, then I also have to believe that he can guide me through the forest.'

They continued walking. He appeared to be wandering aimlessly, from one side to the other, changing direction even when there was no obstacle in his path. More than once they walked in a circle, passing the same place three or four times.

'Perhaps he's testing me.' She was determined to see this experience through to the end and tried telling herself that everything that was happening – including those circular walks – was perfectly normal.

She had come a very long way and had hoped for more from this encounter. Dublin was over 90 miles away, and the buses to the village were uncomfortable and left at absurd times. She'd had to get up early, travel for three hours, ask the people in the village where she might find him and explain what she wanted with such a strange man. Finally, someone had told her in which part of the forest he could usually be found during the day, but not without first warning her that he'd already tried to seduce one of the village girls.

'He's an interesting man,' she thought to herself. They were climbing now, and she found herself hoping that the sun would linger a little longer in the sky. She was afraid she might slip on the damp leaves.

'Why do you really want to learn about magic?'

Brida was pleased that the silence had been broken. She gave him the same answer she had given before.

But he wasn't satisfied.

'Perhaps you want to learn about magic because it's mysterious and secret, because it provides answers that few human beings ever manage to find in a whole lifetime, or perhaps because it evokes a romantic past.'

Brida said nothing. She didn't know what to say. Afraid to give an answer the Magus might not like, she rather wished he would lapse back into his earlier silence.

At last, they came to the top of a hill, having crossed the entire forest. The ground there was rocky and bare of vegetation, but at least it was less slippery, and Brida could follow the Magus without difficulty.

He sat down on the highest point and asked Brida to do the same.

'Other people have been here before,' said the Magus. 'They, too, came to ask me to teach them about magic, but I've taught everything I needed to teach. I've given back to humanity what it gave to me. Now I want to be alone, to climb mountains, tend plants and commune with God.'

'That's not true,' replied the girl.

'What isn't true?' he asked, surprised.

'You might want to commune with God, but it isn't true that you want to be alone.'

Brida regretted having spoken. She had spoken on an impulse and now it was too late to correct her mistake. Perhaps there were people who wanted to be alone. Perhaps women needed men more than men needed women.

The Magus, however, showed no sign of irritation when he spoke again.

'I'm going to ask you a question,' he said, 'and you must be absolutely honest in your answer. If you tell me the truth, I'll teach you what you ask. If you lie, you must never again return to this forest.'

Brida gave a sigh of relief. He was going to ask her a question. She simply had to tell the truth, that was all. She had always assumed that a Teacher would demand really difficult things of someone before taking them on as a pupil.

'Let's suppose that I do start teaching you what I've learned,' he said, his eyes fixed on hers. 'Let's suppose that I start to show you the parallel universes that surround us, the angels, the wisdom of nature, the mysteries of the Tradition of the Sun and the Tradition of the Moon. Then one day, you go into town to buy some food and, in the middle of the street, you meet the love of your life.'

'I wouldn't know how to recognise him,' she thought, but decided to say nothing. This question was turning out to be more difficult than she'd imagined.

'He feels the same and comes over to you. You fall in love with each other. You continue your studies with me. During the day, I teach you the wisdom of the Cosmos, and at night, he teaches you the wisdom of Love. But there comes a moment when those two things can no longer coexist, and you have to choose.'

The Magus paused for a few seconds. Before he actually asked the question, he felt afraid of what the girl's reply might be. Her coming there that evening meant the end of a stage in both their lives. He knew this, because he understood the traditions and intentions of Teachers. He needed her as much as she needed him, but she had to answer the question he put to her truthfully; that was the sole condition.

'Now answer this question with total honesty,' he said at last, screwing up his courage. 'Would you give up everything you had learned until then – all the possibilities and all the mysteries that the world of magic could offer you – in order to stay with the love of your life?'

Brida looked away. Around her lay the mountains and the forests, and down below, the lights in the village were beginning to come on; soon, families would be gathering round the table to have supper. They worked hard and honestly, they feared God, and they tried to help their fellow man. They did all these things because they had known love. Their lives had a reason, they could understand everything that was going on in the universe without ever having heard of things like the Tradition of the Sun and the Tradition of the Moon.

'I see no contradiction between my search and my personal happiness,' she said.

'Answer my question.' His eyes were still fixed on hers. 'Would you give up everything for that man?'

Brida felt a tremendous urge to cry. It wasn't so much a question, it was a choice, the most difficult choice anyone would have to make in life. It was something she'd already thought about a lot. There had been a time when nothing in the world was as important as herself. She'd had several boyfriends and had always believed that she loved each one, only to see love vanish from one moment to the next. Of all the things she'd experienced until then, love had been the most difficult. Just then, she was in love with someone slightly older than herself; he was studying physics and had a completely different vision of the world from hers. Once again, she was putting her belief in love, trusting her feelings, but she'd been disappointed so often before that she was no longer sure of anything. Nevertheless, this was the great gamble of her life.

She continued to avoid the Magus's gaze. Her eyes were fixed on the village and its twinkling lights. People had been trying to understand the universe through love ever since the beginning of time.

'I'd give it all up,' she said at last.

The man standing before her, she thought, would never understand what went on in people's hearts. He was a man who knew the power and the mystery of magic, but he didn't know people. His hair was grizzled, his skin burned by the sun, and he had the physique of someone used to walking in the mountains. He was so very attractive, with eyes that revealed a soul full of answers, and he would once again be disappointed by the feelings of ordinary human beings. She was disappointed with herself too, but she couldn't lie.

'Look at me,' said the Magus.

Brida felt ashamed, but did as he asked.

'You told the truth. I will be your teacher.'

Darkness fell, and the stars were shining in a moonless sky. It took two hours for Brida to tell the stranger her life story. She tried to look for facts that would explain her interest in magic – childhood visions, premonitions, an inner calling – but could find nothing. She simply felt a need to know, that was all. And because of that, she had taken courses in astrology, tarot and numerology.

'Those are merely languages,' said the Magus, 'and they're not the only ones. Magic speaks all the languages of the human heart.'

'So what is magic?' she asked.

Even in the darkness, Brida could sense that the Magus had turned away from her. He was looking up at the sky, absorbed in thought, perhaps in search of an answer.

'Magic is a bridge,' he said at last, 'a bridge that allows you to walk from the visible world over into the invisible world, and to learn the lessons of both those worlds.'

'And how can I learn to cross that bridge?'

'By discovering your own way of crossing it. Everyone has their own way.'

'That's what I came here to find out.'

'There are two forms,' replied the Magus. 'The Tradition of the Sun, which teaches the secrets through space and the world that surrounds us, and the Tradition of the Moon, which teaches through time and the things that are imprisoned in time's memory.'

Brida had understood. The Tradition of the Sun was the night, the trees, the cold gripping her body, the stars in the sky. And the Tradition of the Moon was that man before her now, with the wisdom of the ancestors shining in his eyes.

'I learned the Tradition of the Moon,' said the Magus, as if he could read her thoughts, 'but I was never a Teacher of that Tradition. I am a Teacher of the Tradition of the Sun.'

'Teach me the Tradition of the Sun, then,' said Brida, feeling slightly disconcerted, for she had sensed a note of tenderness in the Magus's voice.

'I will teach you what I have learned, but the Tradition of the Sun has many roads. One must trust in each person's ability to teach him or herself.'

Brida was right. There was a note of tenderness in the Magus's voice. Far from reassuring her, this frightened her.

'I know I'm capable of understanding the Tradition of the Sun,' she said.

The Magus stopped gazing up at the stars and concentrated on the young woman. He knew that she was not quite ready to learn the Tradition of the Sun and yet he must teach it to her. Some pupils choose their Teachers.

'Before our first lesson, I want to remind you of one thing,' he said. 'When you find your path, you must not be afraid. You need to have sufficient courage to make mistakes. Disappointment, defeat and despair are the tools God uses to show us the way.'

'Strange tools,' said Brida. 'They often dissuade people from carrying on.'

The Magus knew the reason for these tools, he had already experienced both in body and soul.

'Teach me the Tradition of the Sun,' she insisted.

The Magus asked Brida to lean back against the rock and relax.

'There's no need to close your eyes. Look at the world around you and try to see and understand as much as you can. The Tradition of the Sun is constantly revealing eternal knowledge to each individual.'

Brida did as the Magus told her to, but she felt he was moving much too fast.

'This is the first and most important lesson,' he said. 'It was created by a Spanish mystic who understood the meaning of faith. His name was St John of the Cross.'

He looked at the girl's eager, trusting face. In his heart, he prayed she would understand what he had to teach her. She was, after all, his Soulmate, even if she didn't yet know it, even if she was still very young and fascinated by the things and the people of this world.

In the darkness, Brida could just make out the shape of the Magus going back into the forest and disappearing among the trees to her left. She was afraid of being left there alone, but tried to remain relaxed. This was her first lesson, and she must not show that she was nervous.

'He accepted me as his pupil. I can't disappoint him.'

She was pleased with herself and, at the same time, surprised at how quickly it had all happened. Not that she had ever doubted her abilities – she was proud of herself and of what had brought her there. She was sure that the Magus was somewhere nearby, watching her reactions, to see if she was capable of learning the first lesson of magic. He had spoken of courage, and so even if she felt afraid – images of the snakes and scorpions that might be living underneath that rock began to rise up from the depths of her imagination – she must be brave. In a while, he would return to teach her the first lesson.

'I'm a strong, determined woman,' she repeated to herself under her breath. She was privileged to be there with that man whom other people either loved or feared. She looked back on the evening they had just spent together and recalled the moment when she had sensed a certain tenderness in his voice. 'Perhaps he found me interesting. Perhaps he even wanted to make love with me.' It wouldn't be a bad experience; there was, however, a strange look in his eyes.

'What an idiotic thing to think.' There she was, in search of something very real – a path to knowledge – and suddenly she was thinking of herself as a mere woman. She tried not to think about it again, and it was then that she realised how much time had passed since the Magus had left her alone.

She felt the beginnings of panic; she had heard contradictory views about that man. Some said he was the most powerful Teacher they'd ever met, capable of changing the direction of the wind, of piercing the clouds, purely by the power of thought. And Brida was as fascinated as everyone else by such prodigies.

Other people, though – people on the fringes of the world of magic, who attended the same courses and classes as she did – assured her that he was a black magician and had once used his powers to destroy a man, because he had fallen in love with the man's wife. And this was why, even though he was a Teacher, he had been condemned to wander the lonely forests.

'Perhaps solitude has made his madness worse,' Brida thought, and again felt the first stirrings of panic. She may have been young, but she knew the harm that loneliness could do to people, especially as they got older. She had met people who had lost the glow of being alive because they could no longer fight against loneliness and had ended up becoming addicted to it. They were, for the most part, people who believed the world to be an undignified, inglorious place, and who spent their evenings and nights talking on and on about the mistakes others had made. They were people whom solitude had made into the judges of the world, whose verdicts were scattered to the four winds for whoever cared to listen. Perhaps the Magus had gone mad with loneliness.

A sudden noise nearby made her jump, and her heart raced. All trace of her earlier confidence vanished. She looked around – nothing. A wave of terror seemed to rise up from her belly and spread through her body.

'I must get a grip on myself,' she thought, but it was impossible. Images of snakes and scorpions and childhood ghosts began to appear before her. Brida was too terrified to stay calm. Another image arose: that of a powerful magician who had made a pact with the Devil and was offering her up as a sacrifice.

'Where are you?' she cried. She didn't care now what impression she made on anyone. She simply wanted to get out of there.

No one answered.

'I want to get out of here! Help me!'

There was only the forest and its strange noises. Brida felt so dizzy with fear she thought she might faint. But she mustn't. Now that she was quite sure he was nowhere around, fainting certainly wouldn't help matters. She must stay in control.

This thought made her aware that there was some part of her struggling to maintain control. 'I mustn't call out,' she said to herself. Her shouts could attract other men who lived in that forest and men who live in forests can be more dangerous than any wild animal.

'I have faith,' she started to say softly. 'I have faith in God, faith in my Guardian Angel, who brought me here, and who remains here with me. I can't explain what he's like, but I know he is near. I will not dash my foot against a stone.'

These last words were from a psalm she had learned as a child, and which she hadn't thought about for years. She had been taught the psalm by her grandmother, who had died quite recently. As soon as she wished her grandmother could be there, she immediately felt a friendly presence.

She was beginning to understand that there was a big difference between danger and fear.

'He that dwelleth in the secret place of the most High ...' that was how the Psalm began. She realised that it was all coming back to her word for word, exactly as if her grandmother were reciting it to her now. She kept reciting for some time, without stopping, and despite her fear, she felt calmer. She had no choice: either she believed in God, in her Guardian Angel, or she despaired.

She felt a protective presence. 'I need to believe in this presence. I don't know how to explain it, but it exists. And it will stay with me all night, because I don't know how to find my way out of here alone.'

When she was a child, she would sometimes wake up in the middle of night, feeling terrified. Her father would carry her to the window and show her the town where they lived. He would talk to her about the nightwatchmen, about the milkman who would already be out delivering the milk, about the baker making their daily bread. Her father was trying to drive out the monsters with which she'd filled the night and replace them with the people who kept watch over the darkness. 'The night is just a part of the day,' he would say.

The night is just a part of the day. Therefore she could feel as safe in the dark as she did in the light. It was the dark that had made her invoke that protective presence. She must trust it. And that trust was called Faith. No one could ever understand Faith, but Faith was what she was experiencing now, an inexplicable immersion in blackest night. It only existed because she believed in it. Miracles couldn't be explained either, but they existed for those who believed in them.

'He did say something about the first lesson,' she thought, suddenly realising what was going on. The protective presence was there because she believed in it. Brida began to feel the fatigue of so many hours under tension. She began to relax again and, with each moment that passed, she felt more protected.

She had faith. And faith wouldn't allow the forest to be peopled again with scorpions and snakes. Faith would keep her Guardian Angel awake and watching.

She leaned back against the rock again and, all unknowing, fell asleep.

It was light when she woke, and a beautiful sun was gilding everything around her. She felt a little cold, her clothes were grubby, but her soul was rejoicing. She had spent the whole night alone in a forest.

She looked everywhere for the Magus, knowing that she would not find him. He must be walking in the forest somewhere trying 'to commune with God', and perhaps wondering if the girl who'd come to see him the previous night had sufficient courage to learn the first lesson of the Tradition of the Sun.

'I learned about the Dark Night,' she said to the now silent forest. 'I learned that the search for God is a Dark Night, that Faith is a Dark Night. And that's hardly a surprise really, because for us each day is a dark night. None of us knows what might happen even the next minute, and yet still we go forwards. Because we trust. Because we have Faith.'

Or, who knows, perhaps because we just don't see the mystery contained in the next second. Not that it mattered. What mattered was knowing that she had understood.

That every moment in life is an act of faith.

That you could choose to fill it with snakes and scorpions or with a strong protecting force.

That Faith cannot be explained. It was simply a Dark Night. And all she had to do was to accept it or not.

Brida looked at her watch and saw that it was getting late. She had to catch a bus, travel for three hours and think up some convincing excuse to give her boyfriend; he would never believe she had spent the whole night alone in a forest.

'It's a very difficult thing, the Tradition of the Sun!' she shouted to the forest. 'I have to be my own Teacher, and that isn't what I was expecting!'

She looked at the village down below, mentally traced her path back through the woods and set off. First, though, she turned to the rock again. In a loud, joyous voice, she cried:

'There's one other thing. You're a very interesting man.'

Leaning against the trunk of an old tree, the Magus watched the girl vanish into the woods. He had listened to her fears and heard her cries during the night. At one point, he had even been tempted to go over and embrace her, to shield her from her terror, saying that she didn't need this kind of challenge.

Now he was pleased that he hadn't, and he felt proud that the girl, in all her youthful confusion, was his Soulmate.

In the centre of Dublin there is a bookshop that specialises in occult studies. It has never advertised in newspapers or magazines; the people who go there do so on the recommendation of others, and the owner is glad to have such a select, specialist clientele.

Even so, the bookshop is always full. Brida had heard about it and finally managed to get the address from the person teaching the course on astral travel she was currently attending. She went there late one afternoon, after work, and was delighted with the place.

From then on, whenever she could, she would go there to look at the books, but she never bought any because they were all imported and very expensive. She would leaf through them, studying the designs and symbols in some of the books, and intuitively tuning in to the vibration of all that accumulated knowledge. She had grown more cautious since her experience with the Magus. Sometimes she would bemoan to herself the fact that she only managed to take part in things she could already understand. She sensed that she was missing out on something very important in life, and that if she carried on as she was, she would simply continue to repeat the same experiences over and over. And yet she didn't have the courage to change. She needed to be constantly struggling to discover her path; now that she had experienced the Dark Night, she knew that she didn't want to find her way through it. And although she was sometimes dissatisfied with herself, she felt unable to go beyond her own limitations.

Books were safer. The shelves contained reprints of treatises written hundreds of years ago; it was an area in which very few people dared to say anything new. And in the pages of these books, occult knowledge, distant and remote, seemed to smile at the efforts made by each generation to uncover it.

Apart from looking at the books, Brida had another important reason for going to the shop – to observe the other customers. Sometimes, she would pretend to be reading some respectable alchemical treatise, when she was, in fact, scrutinising the men and women, usually older than her, who frequented the shop and who knew what they wanted and always went to the right shelf. She tried to imagine what they must be like in private. Some looked very wise, capable of awakening forces and powers of which mere mortals knew nothing. Others appeared to be desperately trying to rediscover answers they had long ago forgotten, but without which life had no meaning.

She noticed, too, that the most regular customers always had a word with the owner. They talked about strange things, such as the phases of the moon, the properties of stones and the correct pronunciation of ritual words.

One afternoon, Brida got up sufficient courage to do the

same. She was on her way back from work, on a day when everything had gone well. She thought she should make the most of that good luck.

'I know that there are secret societies,' she said. She thought this a good conversational opener. She 'knew' something.

But the owner merely looked up from his accounts and stared at her in amazement.

'I was with the Magus in Folk,' said Brida, rather put out now, and not knowing quite how to continue. 'He explained to me about the Dark Night. He told me that the path of wisdom means not being afraid to make mistakes.'

She noticed that the owner was listening more intently now. If the Magus had bothered to teach her something, she must be special.

'If you know that the Dark Night is the path, why do you need books?' he said at last, and she knew that mentioning the Magus had not been a good idea.

'Because that isn't the way I want to learn,' she said.

The owner looked more closely at the young woman standing before him. While she clearly had a Gift, it was nevertheless odd that the Magus of Folk should have devoted so much time to her. There must be something else. She could be lying, but then again she had spoken of the Dark Night.

'You often come here,' he said. 'You arrive, read a few books, but never buy anything.'

'They're too expensive,' said Brida, sensing that he wanted to continue the conversation. 'But I've read other books and I've attended courses.'

She told him the names of her teachers, hoping to impress him still more.

Again things did not go quite as she expected. The owner interrupted her and went to serve another customer who wanted to know if the book he'd ordered had come in, an almanac containing the planetary positions for the next hundred years.

The owner examined various packages stored underneath the counter. Brida saw that the packages bore stamps from all corners of the world.

She was getting more and more nervous. Her initial courage had vanished completely, but she had no option but to wait for the other customer to check that it was the right book, pay for it, receive his change and leave. Only then did the owner turn to her again.

'I don't know how to continue,' said Brida. Her eyes were beginning to fill with tears.

'What are you good at?' asked the owner.

'Going after what I believe in.' That was the only possible reply; she spent her life in pursuit of what she believed in. The only problem was that she believed in something different every day.

The owner wrote a name on the sheet of paper on which he was doing his accounts, tore off the piece he had written on and held it for a moment in his hand.

'I'm going to give you an address,' he said. 'There was a time when people accepted magical experiences as natural. There were no priests then, and no one went chasing after the secrets of the occult.'

Brida wasn't sure whether he was referring to her or not.

'Do you know what magic is?' he asked.

'It's a bridge between the visible world and the invisible world.'

The owner gave her the piece of paper. On it was a phone number and a name: Wicca.

Brida snatched the paper from him, thanked him and left. When she reached the door, she turned and said:

'I also know that magic speaks many languages, even the language of booksellers, who pretend to be unhelpful, but are, in fact, very generous and approachable.'

She blew him a kiss and disappeared. The bookseller paused over his accounts, and stood looking at his shop. 'The Magus of Folk taught her those things,' he thought. A Gift, however good, wasn't reason enough for the Magus to take such an interest. There must be some other motive. Wicca would find it out.

It was time to close the shop. The bookseller had noticed lately that his clientele was starting to change. It was becoming younger. As the old treatises crowding his shelves predicted, things were finally beginning to return to the place from whence they came.

The old building was in the centre of town, in a place that is now only visited by tourists in search of a little nineteenth-century romanticism. Brida had had to wait a week before Wicca would agree to see her, and now she was standing outside a mysterious grey building, struggling to contain her excitement. That building was exactly as she'd imagined it would be; it was just the kind of place where the type of person who visited the bookshop should live.

There was no lift. She went up the stairs slowly so as not to be out of breath when she reached the floor she wanted, and when she arrived, she rang the bell of the only door there.

Inside, a dog barked. Then, after a brief delay, a slim, elegant, serious-looking woman opened the door.

'I phoned earlier,' said Brida.

Wicca indicated that she should come in, and Brida found herself in a living room entirely painted in white and with examples of modern art everywhere – with paintings on the walls and sculptures and vases on the tables. The light from outside was filtered through white curtains. The room was cleverly divided into different areas to accommodate sofas, dining table and a well-stocked library. Everything was in the very best taste and reminded Brida of the architecture and design magazines she used to look at on the newstands.

'It must have cost a fortune,' she thought.

Wicca led Brida into the vast living room, into an area furnished by two Italian armchairs in leather and steel. Between the two chairs was a low glass table with steel legs.

'You're very young,' said Wicca at last.

There was little point in making her usual comment about ballerinas, and so Brida said nothing, waiting to hear what the woman would say next and meanwhile wondering what such a modern design was doing inside an old building like that. Her romantic idea of the search for knowledge had once again been shaken.

'He phoned me,' Wicca said, and Brida understood that she was referring to the bookseller.

'I came in search of a Teacher. I want to follow the road of magic.'

Wicca looked at Brida. She clearly possessed a Gift, but she needed to know why the Magus of Folk had been so interested in her. The Gift on its own was not enough. If the Magus had been new to magic, he might have been impressed by the clarity with which the Gift manifested itself in the young woman, but he had lived long enough to know that everyone possesses a Gift. He was wise to such traps.

She got up, went over to one of the bookshelves and picked up her favourite deck of cards.

'Do you know how to lay the cards?' she asked.

Brida nodded. She had done a few courses and knew that the deck in the woman's hand was a tarot deck, with seventy-eight cards. She had learned various ways of laying out the tarot and was glad to have a chance to show off her knowledge.

However, the woman kept hold of the deck. She shuffled the cards, then placed them face down, in no particular order, on the glass table. This was a method quite unlike any Brida had learned on her courses. The woman sat looking at them for a moment, said a few words in a strange language, then turned over just one of the cards.

It was card number 23. A king of clubs.

'Good protection,' she said. 'From a strong, powerful man with dark hair.'

Her boyfriend was neither strong nor powerful, and the Magus's hair was grey.

'Don't think about his physical appearance,' said Wicca, as if she had read her thoughts. 'Think of your Soulmate.'

'What do you mean "Soulmate"?' Brida was surprised. The woman inspired a strange respect, different from the respect she had felt for the Magus or for the bookseller.

Wicca did not answer the question. She again shuffled the cards, and again spread them in that same disorderly manner on the table, except that this time the cards were face up. The card in the middle of that apparent confusion was card number 11. A woman forcing open the mouth of a lion.

Wicca picked up the card and asked Brida to hold it. Brida did so, although without knowing quite what was required of her.

'In previous incarnations, your stronger side was always a woman,' Wicca said.

'What do you mean by "Soulmate"?' Brida asked again. It was the first time she had challenged the woman, but it was, nonetheless, a very timid challenge.

Wicca remained silent for a moment. A suspicion crossed her mind – for some reason the Magus had not taught the girl about Soulmates. 'Nonsense,' she said to herself and brushed the thought aside.

'The Soulmate is the first thing people learn about when they want to follow the Tradition of the Moon,' she said. 'Only by understanding the Soulmate can we understand how knowledge can be transmitted over time.'

As Wicca continued her explanation, Brida remained silent, feeling anxious.

'We are eternal because we are all manifestations of God,' Wicca said. 'That is why we go through many lives and many deaths, emerging out of some unknown place and going towards another equally unknown place. You must get used to the fact that there are many things in magic which are not and never will be explained. God decided to do certain things in a certain way and why He did this is a secret known only to Him.'

'The Dark Night of Faith,' thought Brida. So it existed in the Tradition of the Moon as well.

'The fact is that this happens,' Wicca went on. 'And when people think of reincarnation, they always come up against a very difficult question: if, in the beginning, there were so few people on the face of the Earth, and now there are so many, where did all those new souls come from?'

Brida held her breath. She had asked herself this question many times.

'The answer is simple,' said Wicca, after pausing to savour the young woman's eager silence. 'In certain reincarnations, we divide into two. Our souls divide as do crystals and stars, cells and plants.

'Our soul divides in two, and those new souls are in turn transformed into two and so, within a few generations, we are scattered over a large part of Earth.'

'And does only one of those parts know who it is?' asked Brida. She had many questions to ask, but she wanted to ask them one at a time, and this seemed the most important.

'We form part of what the alchemists call the *Anima mundi*, the Soul of the World,' said Wicca, without replying to the question. 'The truth is that if the *Anima mundi* were merely to keep dividing, it would keep growing, but it would also become gradually weaker. That is why, as well as dividing into two, we also find ourselves. And that process of finding ourselves is called Love. Because when a soul divides, it always divides into a male part and a female part.

'That's how the Book of Genesis explains it: the soul of Adam was split in two, and Eve was born out of him.'

Wicca stopped suddenly and sat looking at the cards scattered on the table.

'There are many cards,' she said, 'but they're all part of the same deck. In order to understand their message, we need them all, all are equally important. So it is with souls. Human beings are all interlinked, like the cards in this deck.

'In each life, we feel a mysterious obligation to find at least one of those Soulmates. The Greater Love that separated them feels pleased with the Love that brings them together again.'

'But how will I know who my Soulmate is?' Brida felt that this was one of the most important questions she had ever asked in her life.

Wicca laughed. She had already asked herself that question and with the same eager anxiety as the young woman opposite her. You could tell your Soulmate by the light in their eyes, and since time began, that has been how people have recognised their true love. The Tradition of the Moon used a different process: a kind of vision that showed a point of light above the left shoulder of your Soulmate. But she wouldn't tell the girl that just yet; she might one day learn to see that point of light, or she might not. She would get her answer soon enough.

'By taking risks,' she said to Brida. 'By risking failure, disappointment, disillusion, but never ceasing in your search for Love. As long as you keep looking, you will triumph in the end.'

Brida remembered the Magus saying something similar when he spoke about the path of magic. 'Perhaps it's all the same thing,' she thought.

Wicca started picking up the cards from the table, and Brida sensed that her time was nearly up. Yet there was one other question to ask.

'Is it possible to meet more than one Soulmate in each life?'

'Yes,' thought Wicca with a certain bitterness. And when that happens, the heart is divided, and the result is pain and suffering. Yes, we can meet three or four Soulmates, because we are many and we are scattered. The young woman was asking the right questions, but she had to avoid answering them.

'The essence of Creation is one and one alone,' she said. 'And that essence is called Love. Love is the force that brings us back together, in order to condense the experience dispersed in many lives and many parts of the world.

'We are responsible for the whole Earth because we do not know where they might be, those Soulmates we were from the beginning of time. If they are well, then we, too, will be happy. If they are not well, we will suffer, however unconsciously, a portion of their pain. Above all, though, we are responsible for re-encountering, at least once in every incarnation, the Soulmate who is sure to cross our path. Even if it is only for a matter of moments, because those moments bring with them a Love so intense that it justifies the rest of our days.'

The dog barked in the kitchen. Wicca finished picking up the cards and looked again at Brida.

'We can also allow our Soulmate to pass us by, without accepting him or her, or even noticing. Then we will need another incarnation in order to find that Soulmate. And because of our selfishness, we will be condemned to the worst torture humankind ever invented for itself: loneliness.'

Wicca got up and showed Brida to the door.

'You didn't come here to find out about your Soulmate,' she said, before saying goodbye. 'You have a Gift, and once I know what that Gift is, I might be able to teach you the Tradition of the Moon.'

Brida felt very special. She needed to feel this, for the woman inspired a respect she had felt for very few other people.

'I'll do my best. I want to learn the Tradition of the Moon.'

36

'Because,' she thought, 'the Tradition of the Moon doesn't require you to spend the night alone in a dark forest.'

'Now listen to me,' said Wicca sternly. 'Every day from today, at an hour of your choosing, sit down alone at a table and spread the tarot deck as I did, completely at random. Don't try to understand anything. Simply study the cards. They will teach you all you need to know for the moment.'

'It's like the Tradition of the Sun: me teaching myself again,' thought Brida as she went down the stairs. And only when she was on the bus did she realise that the woman had spoken of a Gift. But she could talk about that at their next meeting.

For a whole week, Brida devoted half an hour a day to spreading the tarot cards on the table in the living room. She went to bed at ten o'clock and set the alarm for one in the morning. She would get up, make a quick cup of coffee, and sit down to contemplate the cards, trying to decipher their hidden language.

The first night, she was very excited. Brida was convinced that Wicca had taught her some kind of secret ritual and so she tried to spread the cards in exactly the same way, expecting some occult message to be revealed. After half an hour, apart from a few minor visions, which she felt were merely the fruits of her imagination, nothing of any great note had happened.

She did the same thing on the second night. Wicca had said that the cards would tell their own story and, to judge by the courses Brida had attended, it was a very ancient story indeed, dating back more than three thousand years, to a time when mankind was closer to the original wisdom.

'The pictures seem so simple,' she thought. A woman

forcing open the mouth of a lion, a cart pulled by two mysterious animals, a man sitting before a table covered with sundry objects. She had been taught that the deck was a book, a book in which the Divine Wisdom had noted down the main changes that take place during our journey through life. But its author, knowing that humanity learned more easily from vice than from virtue, had arranged for this sacred book to be transmitted across the generations in the form of a game. The deck was an invention of the gods.

'It can't be that simple,' thought Brida, every time she spread the cards on the table. She had been taught complicated methods, elaborate systems, and those cards arranged in no particular order began to have a troubling effect on her reasoning. On the third night, she threw the cards down angrily on the floor. For a moment, she thought that this angry reaction might have some magical inspiration behind it, but the results were equally unsatisfactory, just a few indefinable intuitions, which, again, she dismissed as mere imaginings.

At the same time, the idea of her Soulmate didn't leave her for a moment. At first, she felt as if she were going back to her adolescence, to dreams of an enchanted prince crossing mountains and valleys in search of his lady of the glass slipper or in order to awaken a sleeping beauty with a kiss. 'Finding your Soulmate is something that only happens in fairy tales,' she told herself, half-joking. Fairy tales had been her first experience of the magical universe that she was now so eager to enter, and more than once she had wondered why people ended up distancing themselves from that world, knowing the immense joy that childhood had brought to their lives.

'Perhaps because they weren't content with feeling joy.' She found the idea slightly absurd, but nevertheless recorded it in her diary as a 'creative' thought.

After spending a week obsessed with the idea of the Soulmate, Brida became gripped by a terrifying feeling: what if she chose the wrong man? On the eighth night, when she woke again to carry out her vain contemplation of the tarot cards, she decided to invite her boyfriend out to supper the following night.

$\mathcal{S}$he chose a fairly inexpensive restaurant, because he always insisted on paying the bill, despite the fact that he earned far less as a research assistant to a physics professor at the university than she earned as a secretary. It was still summer, and they sat out at one of the tables on the pavement, by the river.

'I want to know when the spirits are going to let me sleep with you again,' said Lorens good-humouredly.

Brida looked at him tenderly. She had asked him not to come to her apartment for two weeks, and he had agreed, protesting just warmly enough for her to know how much he loved her. In his way, he, too, was seeking to understand the mysteries of the Universe, and if, one day, he were to ask her to stay away from him for two weeks, she would have to say 'Yes'.

They dined unhurriedly and largely in silence, watching the boats crossing the river and the people walking past on the pavement. The bottle of white wine on the table was emptied and replaced by another. Half an hour later, they had pushed their two chairs together and were sitting, arms around each other, gazing up at the starry summer sky.

'Just look at that sky,' said Lorens, stroking her hair. 'What we're looking at now is how the sky would have appeared thousands of years ago.'

He had told her the same thing on the day they first met, but Brida chose not to interrupt him – this was his way of sharing his world with her.

'Many of those stars have already died, and yet their light still fills the Universe. Other stars were born far away, and their light has not yet reached us.'

'So no one knows what the real sky looks like?' She had asked that same question on their first meeting too, but it was good to repeat such delicious moments.

'We don't know. We study what we can see, but what we see is not always what exists.'

'I want to ask you something. What are we made of? Where did the atoms that make up our bodies come from?'

Lorens looked up at the ancient sky and said:

'They were created along with these stars and this river. In the first second of the Universe's existence.'

'So after that first moment of Creation, nothing more was added.'

'No, nothing. Everything moved and continues to move. Everything was transformed and continues to be transformed. But all the matter that exists in the Universe now is the same matter from all those billions of years ago, and not so much as a single atom has been added.'

Brida sat studying the movement of both river and stars. It was easy to see the river flowing across the Earth, but it was hard to see the stars moving in the sky. And yet both were moving.

'Lorens,' she said at last, after a long silence during which they both watched a boat passing. 'Let me ask what might seem an absurd question: is it physically possible that the atoms that make up my body could have been in the body of someone who lived before me?'

Lorens stared at her in amazement.

'What do you mean?'

'What I said. Is such a thing possible?'

'They could be in plants or insects or they could have turned into helium molecules and be out there somewhere, millions of miles from Earth.'

'But is it possible that the atoms that made up the body of someone who died could be in my body and in someone else's body?'

He said nothing for a moment, then said:

'Yes, it is.'

The sound of distant music reached them. It came from a barge crossing the river, and even from far away, Brida could make out the silhouette of a sailor framed in a lighted window. It was a tune that reminded her of her adolescence; it brought back memories of school dances, the smell of her bedroom, the colour of the ribbon she used to use to tie up her pony-tail. Brida realised that Lorens had never before considered the question she had asked him, and was perhaps, at that moment, wondering if his own body contained the atoms of Viking warriors, of volcanic explosions, or of prehistoric animals that had mysteriously disappeared.

But her thoughts were elsewhere. All she wanted to know was this: had the man so tenderly embracing her once been part of herself?

The barge came closer and the music began to fill the air around them. Conversations on the other tables stopped too, everyone eager to find out where the sound was coming from, because everyone had once been an adolescent, attended school dances and had dreams full of stories about warriors and fairies.

'I love you, Lorens.'

And Brida hoped against hope that this young man who knew so much about the light from the stars contained a little of the person she had once been.

I t's no good, I can't do it.'
Brida sat up in bed and felt for the packet of cigarettes on the bedside table. Going against all her normal habits, she decided to smoke a cigarette before breakfast.

It was another two days until she was due to meet Wicca again. She knew that, during the last two weeks, she had tried her hardest. She had channelled all her hopes into the method of spreading the cards taught to her by that attractive and mysterious woman and she had struggled hard not to disappoint her, but the cards refused to reveal their secrets.

Each time she had finished the exercise on the previous three nights, she had felt like crying. She felt vulnerable and alone and had a sense that a great opportunity was slipping through her fingers. Once again, she felt that life was not treating her as it treated other people: it gave her every chance to achieve something, and just when she was close to her objective, the ground opened up and swallowed her. That's how it had been with her studies, with certain boyfriends, with certain dreams she had never shared with anyone.

She thought of the Magus. Perhaps he could help her. But she had promised herself that she would only go back to Folk when she knew enough about magic to face him again.

And now it seemed that this would never happen.

She lay for a long time in bed, before deciding to get up and make breakfast. Finally, she screwed up the necessary resolve and courage to face another day, one more of her 'daily Dark Nights' as she had taken to calling them since her experience in the forest. She prepared some coffee, looked at her watch and saw that she still had enough time.

She went over to the shelf and searched among the books for the piece of paper the bookseller had given her. To console herself she thought: there are other paths. She had met the Magus, she had met Wicca, and she would, in the end, meet the person who could teach her in a way that she could understand.

But she knew this was merely an excuse.

'I'm always starting things and then giving up,' she thought rather sourly. Perhaps life would soon realise this and stop presenting her with the same opportunities over and over. Or perhaps, by always giving up when she had only just started, she had exhausted all possible paths without even taking a single step.

But that was how she was, and she felt herself growing gradually weaker and less and less able to change. A few years before, she would have felt depressed by her own behaviour, but she would, at least, still have been capable of the occasional heroic gesture; now, though, she was starting to adapt to her own mistakes. She knew other people who did the same – they, too, got used to their mistakes and it wasn't long before they began to see them as virtues. And by then it was too late.

She considered not phoning Wicca and simply disappearing. But what about the bookshop? She wouldn't then have the courage to go there again. If she just disappeared, the bookseller would not be so kind next time. 'It's happened before. Because of some thoughtless gesture towards one person, I've ended up losing touch with other people I really cared about.' She couldn't do the same thing now. She was on a path where valuable contacts were very hard to find.

She steeled herself and dialled the number on the piece of paper. Wicca answered.

'I won't be able to come tomorrow,' said Brida.

'No, the plumber can't make it either,' replied Wicca. For a moment Brida had no idea what the woman was talking about.

Then Wicca started complaining about some problem with her kitchen sink and how she'd arranged several times for a man to come and fix it, but he never came. She launched into a long story about old buildings, which might look terribly imposing but which were, of course, beset by all kinds of problems. Then, in the middle of her story about the plumber, Wicca suddenly asked:

'Have you got your tarot cards handy?'

Surprised, Brida said that she did. Wicca asked her to spread the cards on the table, because she was going to teach her a method of finding out whether the plumber would or would not turn up the following day.

Feeling even more surprised, Brida did as she was asked. She spread the cards and sat staring blankly at the table while she awaited instructions from the other end of the line. The courage to explain the reason for her phone call was gradually fading.

Wicca was still talking, and Brida decided to listen to her patiently. Perhaps she would become her friend. Perhaps then she would be more tolerant and show her easier ways of understanding the Tradition of the Moon.

Wicca, meanwhile, was weaving one topic of conversation seamlessly into another, and having finished her litany of complaints about plumbers, she started describing an argument she'd had with the building manager about the caretaker's salary. She then moved on to a report that she'd read on old-age pensions.

Brida accompanied all this with a few affirmative grunts, agreeing with everything Wicca was saying, but no longer listening. A terrible tedium took hold of her. This conversation with a woman she barely knew regarding plumbers, caretakers and pensioners, at that hour in the morning, was one of the most boring things she'd ever experienced. She kept trying to distract herself with the cards on the table, finding little details that she'd never noticed before.

Now and then, Wicca would ask if she was still listening and she'd give a mumbled 'Yes'. But her mind was miles away, travelling, wandering about in places she'd never been to before. Every detail on the cards seemed to push her further on in that journey.

All of a sudden, like someone entering a dream, Brida realised that she could no longer hear what Wicca was saying.

A voice, a voice that seemed to come from within – but which she knew came from outside – began to whisper something to her. 'Do you understand?' Brida said that she did. 'Do you understand?' asked the mysterious voice again.

This, however, was of no importance. The tarot cards before her began to show fantastic scenes: men with bronzed, oiled bodies, wearing only thongs, and some sporting masks like the giant heads of fish. Clouds raced across the sky, as if everything were moving much faster than normal, and the scene shifted abruptly to a square, surrounded by grand buildings, where a few old men were urgently telling secrets to a group of young boys, as if some form of very ancient knowledge were about to be lost for ever.

'Add seven and eight and you'll have my number. I'm the devil, and I signed the book,' said a boy in medieval clothes at what appeared to be a celebration. Drunken men and women smiled out at her. The scene changed yet again to the sea, to reveal temples carved out of the rocks, and then the sky began to be covered by black clouds pierced by brilliant flashes of lightning.

A door appeared. It was a heavy door, like the door of an old castle. The door came closer to Brida, and she had a sense that soon she would be able to open it.

'Come back,' said the voice.

'Come back,' said the voice on the phone. It was Wicca. Brida was annoyed with her for interrupting such a remarkable experience merely to bore her with more talk about caretakers and plumbers.

'Just a moment,' she replied. She was struggling to find that door, but everything had vanished.

'I know what happened,' Wicca told her. Brida was stunned, in a state of shock. She couldn't understand what was going on.

'I know what happened,' Wicca said again, in response to Brida's silence. 'I won't say anything more about the plumber. He was here last week and fixed everything.'

Before hanging up, she said she would expect Brida at the agreed time.

Brida put down the phone without saying goodbye. She sat for a long time staring at the kitchen wall before subsiding into convulsive, soothing sobs.

It was a trick,' Wicca told a frightened Brida, when they sat down again in the Italian armchairs.

'I know how you must be feeling,' she went on. 'Sometimes we set off down a path simply because we don't believe in it. It's easy enough. All we have to do then is prove that it isn't the right path for us. However, when things start to happen, and the path does reveal itself to us, we become afraid of carrying on.'

Wicca said that she didn't understand why so many people chose to spend their whole life destroying paths they didn't even want to follow, instead of following the one path that would lead them somewhere.

'I can't believe it was a trick,' protested Brida. She had lost her air of arrogance and defiance. Her respect for Wicca had grown considerably.

'No, no, the vision wasn't a trick. The trick I'm referring to is the phone. For millions of years, we only ever spoke to someone we could see, then, in less than a century, "seeing" and "speaking" were suddenly separated. We think it's quite normal now and don't realise the huge impact it has on our reflexes. Our body still hasn't got used to it.

'The practical result is that, when we speak on the phone, we often enter a state very similar to certain magical trances. Our mind tunes into another frequency and becomes more receptive to the invisible world. I know some witches who always keep a pen and paper by the phone and, while they're talking to someone, they sit doodling apparently nonsensical things. When they hang up, though, they find that their "doodles" are often symbols from the Tradition of the Moon.'

'But why did the tarot reveal itself to me?'

'That's the great problem with anyone wanting to study magic,' replied Wicca. 'When we set out on the path, we always have a fairly clear idea of what we hope to find. Women are generally seeking their Soulmate, and men are looking for Power. Neither party is really interested in learning. They simply want to reach the thing they have set as their goal.

'But the path of magic – like the path of life – is and always will be the path of Mystery. Learning something means coming into contact with a world of which you know nothing. In order to learn, you must be humble.'

'Like plunging into the Dark Night,' said Brida.

'Don't interrupt.' There was a note of barely contained irritation in Wicca's voice, but Brida realised that it wasn't because of what she'd said. 'Maybe she's angry with the Magus,' she thought. 'Perhaps she was once in love with him. They are more or less the same age.'

'I'm sorry,' she said.

'That's all right.' Wicca seemed equally surprised by her own reaction.

'You were telling me about the tarot.'

'When you were spreading the cards, you always had a preconceived idea of what would happen. You never let the cards tell their own story; you were trying to make them confirm what you imagined you knew.

'I realised this when we started talking on the phone. I realised, too, that it was a sign and that the phone was my ally. So I launched into a very boring conversation and asked you to look at the cards. You went into the trance provoked by the phone, and the cards led you into their magical world.'

Wicca suggested that next time Brida was with someone who was talking on the phone, she should take a good look at their eyes. She would be surprised by what she saw.

want to ask something else,' said Brida over tea in Wicca's surprisingly modern and practical kitchen.

'I want to know why you didn't let me abandon the path.'

'Because,' thought Wicca, 'I want to find out what the Magus saw in you, apart, I mean, from your Gift.' What she said was: 'Because you have a Gift.'

'How do you know?'

'Easy. By your ears.'

'By my ears! How disappointing!' Brida thought to herself. 'And there was me thinking she could see my aura.'

'Everyone has a Gift, but some are born with a more highly developed Gift than others – me, for example – who have to struggle really hard to develop their Gift. People who were born with a Gift have very small, attached earlobes.'

Instinctively, Brida touched her earlobes. It was true.

'Do you have a car?'

No, Brida said, she didn't.

'Then prepare to spend a fortune on taxi fares,' said Wicca, getting up. 'It's time to take our next step.'

'Things are suddenly moving very fast,' thought Brida, as she got to her feet. Life was beginning to resemble the clouds she had seen in her trance.

By around mid-afternoon they had reached some mountains about fifteen miles south of Dublin. 'We could have made the same trip by bus,' Brida grumbled to herself while she paid the taxi. Wicca had brought with her a bag and some clothes.

'If you like, I can wait,' said the driver. 'It's going to be pretty difficult finding another taxi in these parts. This is the middle of nowhere.'

'Don't worry,' said Wicca, to Brida's relief. 'We always get what we want.'

The driver gave them a strange look and drove off. They were standing before a grove of trees, which extended as far as the foot of the nearest mountain.

'Ask permission to enter,' said Wicca. 'The spirits of the forests always appreciate good manners.'

Brida asked permission. The wood, which had, up until then, been just an ordinary wood, seemed suddenly to come to life.

'Stay on the bridge between the visible and the invisible,' said Wicca, while they walked through the trees. 'Everything in the Universe has life, and you must always try to stay in contact with that life. It understands your language. And the world will begin to take on a different meaning for you.'

Brida was surprised at Wicca's agility. Her feet seemed to levitate above the ground, making almost no noise.

They reached a clearing, near a huge stone. While she tried to think how that stone could have got there, Brida noticed the ashes from a fire right in the middle of the open space.

It was a beautiful place. It would still be some hours before evening, and the sun shone with the warm gold of summer afternoons. Birds were singing, and a light breeze rustled in the leaves. They were quite high up, and she could look across and down at the horizon.

Wicca took a kind of cloak out of her bag and put it on over her clothes. Then she placed the bag near the trees, so that it couldn't be seen from the clearing.

'Sit down,' she said.

Wicca was somehow different. Brida couldn't decide whether it was the cloak or the profound respect that the place inspired in her.

'First of all, I must explain what I'm going to do. I'm going to find out how the Gift manifests itself in you. I can only begin to teach you once I know something about your Gift.'

Wicca asked Brida to try and relax, to surrender herself to the beauty of the place, just as she had when she had surrendered to the tarot cards.

'At some point in one of your past lives, you set out along the road of magic. I know this from the tarot visions that you described.'

Brida closed her eyes, but Wicca asked her to open them again.

'Magical places are always beautiful and deserve to be contemplated. Waterfalls, mountains and forests are all places where the spirits of Earth tend to play and laugh and speak to us. You are in a sacred place, and it is showing you the birds and the wind. Thank God for this, for the birds, the wind, and for the spirits who inhabit this wood. Always stay on the bridge between the visible and the invisible.'

Wicca's voice was making Brida feel more and more relaxed. She felt an almost religious respect for the moment.

'The other day, I spoke to you about one of the great secrets of magic: the Soulmate. The whole of man's life on the face of Earth can be summed up by that search for his Soulmate. He may pretend to be running after wisdom, money or power, but none of that matters. Whatever he achieves will be incomplete if he fails to find his Soulmate.

'With the exception of a few creatures who are descended from the angels – and who need solitude in order to encounter God – the rest of humanity will only achieve Union with God if, at some point, at some moment in their life, they manage to commune with their Soulmate.'

Brida noticed a strange energy in the air. For a few moments, and for some reason she could not explain, her eyes filled with tears.

'In the Night of Time, when we were separated, one of those parts was charged with nurturing and maintaining knowledge:

man. He went on to understand agriculture, nature and the movements of the stars in the sky. Knowledge was always the power that kept the Universe in its place and the stars turning in their orbits. That was the glory of man – to nurture and maintain knowledge. And that is why the whole human race has survived.

'To women was given something far more subtle and fragile, but without which knowledge makes no sense at all, and that thing was transformation. The men left the soil fertile, we sowed seeds, and the soil was transformed into trees and plants.

'The soil needs the seed, and the seed needs the soil. The one only has meaning with the other. It is the same thing with human beings. When male knowledge joins with female transformation, then the great magical union is created, and its name is Wisdom. Wisdom means both to know and to transform.'

Brida noticed that the wind was growing stronger and that Wicca's voice was leading her again into a trance. The spirits of the forest seemed alive and intent.

'Lie down,' said Wicca.

Brida leaned back and stretched out her legs. Up above her glowed a deep, blue, cloudless sky.

'Go in search of your Gift. I can't go with you today, but don't be afraid. The more you understand yourself, the more you will understand the world. And the closer you will be to your Soulmate.'

Wicca knelt down and looked at the young woman. 'She's just as I once was,' she thought fondly. 'In search of a meaning for everything and capable of looking at the world as did the strong, confident women of old, who were quite happy to rule over their own communities.'

At that time, however, God had been a woman. Wicca bent over Brida's body and unbuckled the belt of Brida's jeans, then half-unzipped them. Brida's muscles tensed.

'Don't worry,' said Wicca affectionately.

She lifted up Brida's T-shirt to reveal her navel. Then she took from the pocket of her cloak a quartz crystal and placed it on Brida's navel.

'Now I want you to close your eyes,' she said softly. 'I want you to imagine the colour of the sky, but keep your eyes closed.'

She took from her cloak a small amethyst and placed it between Brida's closed eyes.

'From now on, do exactly as I tell you and don't worry about anything else. You are in the centre of the Universe. You can see the stars all around you and some of the brighter planets. Experience this landscape as something that wraps about you completely and not like a picture or a screen. Take pleasure in contemplating this Universe; there's no need to worry about anything else. Simply concentrate on your own pleasure. Without any feelings of guilt.'

Brida saw the starry Universe and realised that she could step into it even while she was listening to Wicca's voice. The voice asked her to imagine a vast cathedral in the middle of the Universe. Brida duly saw a Gothic cathedral made of dark stone and which, absurd though it might seem, appeared to form part of the surrounding Universe.

'Walk over to the cathedral and up the steps. Go inside.'

Brida did as Wicca ordered. She went up the cathedral steps, conscious of her bare feet on the cold stone floor. At one point, she had a feeling that there was someone with her, and Wicca's voice seemed to emerge from a person walking behind her. 'I'm imagining things,' thought Brida, and suddenly remembered what she'd been told about the bridge between the visible and the invisible. She mustn't feel afraid of disappointment or failure.

Brida was now standing in front of the cathedral door. It was an enormous wrought-iron affair, adorned with scenes from the lives of the saints, and totally different from the one she had seen on her journey through the tarot cards.

'Open the door and go in.'

Brida felt the cold metal of the handle beneath her hand. Despite the door's great size, it opened easily. She entered and found herself inside a vast church.

'Notice everything around you,' said Wicca. Although it was dark outside, light came streaming in through the cathedral's huge stained-glass windows. She could make out the pews, the side altars, the decorated columns and a few lit candles. Yet everything seemed somehow empty and abandoned. The pews were covered in dust.

'Walk over to your left. Somewhere you will find another door, but this time, it will be a very small one.'

Brida walked through the cathedral. She was aware of the unpleasant feeling of the dusty floor beneath her bare feet. Somewhere, a friendly voice was guiding her. She knew it was Wicca, but she knew, too, that she no longer had any control over her imagination. She was conscious and yet she could not disobey what was being asked of her.

She found the door.

'Go in. There's a spiral staircase leading down.'

Brida had to crouch to get through the door. The walls of the staircase were lined with torches fixed to the wall, illuminating the steps. The steps were very clean. Someone had clearly been there before in order to light the torches.

'You are setting off in search of your past lives. In the cellar of this cathedral is a library. That's where we're going now. I'll be waiting at the foot of the staircase.'

Brida kept going down and down, for how long she didn't know. It made her slightly dizzy. When she did finally reach the bottom, Wicca was there in her cloak. It would be easier now; she felt more protected. She was still deep in her trance.

Wicca opened another door opposite the stairs.

'I'm going to leave you alone here. I'll be outside, waiting. Choose a book and it will show you what you need to know.'

Brida didn't even notice that Wicca was no longer there. She was staring at the dusty tomes. 'I really should come here more often and give everything a good clean.' Her past was grubby and neglected, and she felt sad to think that she'd never read any of these books before. Perhaps they contained important, long-forgotten lessons that she could incorporate into her life.

She looked at the books on the shelf. 'All those lives,' she thought. If she was so very ancient, she really should be wiser. She wished she could read them all, but she didn't have much time, and she must trust in her intuition. She could come back whenever she wanted, now that she knew the way.

She stood for a while not knowing which book to choose. Then she chose one almost at random. It was a fairly slim volume, and Brida took it and sat down on the floor.

She placed the book on her lap, but felt afraid she might open it and find that nothing happened, afraid that she might not be able to read what was written there.

'I need to take risks. I need to feel the fear of failing,' she thought as she opened the book. As soon as she glanced at the pages, she began to feel ill and dizzy again.

'I'm going to faint,' she managed to think before everything went dark.

$\mathcal{S}$he woke with water dripping on her face. She'd had a strange, incomprehensible dream about cathedrals floating in the air and libraries crammed with books. And yet she had never been in a library.

'Loni, are you all right?'

No, she wasn't. She couldn't feel her right foot and she knew this was a bad sign. She didn't feel like talking either, because she didn't want to forget the dream.

'Loni, wake up.'

She must be feverish, delirious, and yet what she saw in her delirium seemed so intensely real. She wished the person who kept calling to her would stop, because the dream was now fast disappearing before she had managed to grasp its meaning.

The sky was cloudy, and the clouds were so low they almost touched the castle's tallest tower. She lay looking up at the clouds. It was just as well she couldn't see the stars; according to the priests, not even the stars were entirely good.

The rain had stopped shortly before she opened her eyes. Loni was pleased it had rained, for that meant the castle's water butts would be full. She slowly shifted her gaze from the clouds to the tower, to the bonfires in the courtyard and the bewildered crowds of people milling around.

'Talbo,' she said softly.

He put his arms around her. She felt the cold of his armour and the smell of soot in his hair.

'How much time has passed? What day is it?'

'You've been asleep for three days,' said Talbo.

She looked at Talbo and felt sorry for him. He was thinner, his face grimy, his skin dull. Not that any of this mattered – she loved him.

'I'm thirsty, Talbo.'

'There's no water. The French found the secret passageway.'

Again she heard the Voices inside her head. For a long time, she had hated those Voices. Her husband was a warrior, a mercenary, who spent most of the year away fighting, and she had always been afraid that the Voices would tell her that he had died in battle. She had found a way of keeping the Voices from speaking to her. She just had to concentrate her mind on an ancient tree near her village. The Voices stopped when she did that. Now, however, she was too weak, and the Voices had returned.

'You're going to die,' said the Voices. 'But he will be saved.'

'But it rained, Talbo,' she said. 'I need water.'

'It was only a few drops. Nothing like enough.'

Loni again looked up at the clouds. They had been there all week, and had done nothing but block the sun, making the winter even colder and the castle even gloomier. Perhaps the French Catholics were right. Perhaps God *was* on their side.

A few mercenaries came over to them. There were fires burning everywhere, and Loni had the sudden feeling that she was in hell.

'The priests are gathering everyone together, sir,' one of them said to Talbo.

'We were hired to fight, not to die,' said another.

'The French have offered us terms of surrender,' replied Talbo. 'They say that those who convert back to the Catholic faith can leave unharmed.'

'The Perfect Ones will not accept,' the Voices whispered to Loni. She knew that. She knew the Perfect Ones well. They were the reason she was there and not at home, where she usually waited for Talbo to return from battle. The Perfect Ones had been besieged in that castle for four months, and during that time, the village women had used the secret passageway connecting village and castle to bring in food, clothes and ammunition; during that time, they had been able to see their husbands, and it was because of them that the fighting had continued. Now, however, the secret passage had been discovered, and she could not go back to the village, nor could any of the other women.

She tried to sit up. Her foot didn't hurt any more. The Voices were telling her that this was a bad sign.

'We have nothing to do with their God. We're not going to die over that, sir,' said another soldier.

A gong began to sound inside the castle. Talbo got to his feet.

'Please, take me with you,' she implored. Talbo looked at his companions and then at the woman who lay trembling before him. For a moment, he didn't know what to do. His men were accustomed to war, and they knew that warriors who were in love usually hid during battles.

'I'm going to die, Talbo. Take me with you, please.'

One of the mercenaries glanced at Talbo.

'She shouldn't be left here alone,' he said. 'The French might start firing again.'

Talbo pretended to agree. He knew that the French would do no such thing. A truce had been called in order to negotiate the surrender of Monségur. But the mercenary understood what was going on in Talbo's heart; he, too, must be a man in love.

'He knows you're going to die,' the Voices said to Loni, while Talbo gently picked her up. Loni didn't want to listen to what the Voices were saying; she was remembering a day when they'd walked along together just like that, through a wheatfield, on a summer afternoon. She had been thirsty then as well, and they had drunk water from a mountain stream.

A crowd of men, soldiers, women and children were gathered round the great rock that formed part of the western wall of the fortress of Monségur. An oppressive silence hung in the air, and Loni knew that this was not out of respect for the priests, but out of fear for what might happen.

The priests arrived. There were a great many of them, all wearing black cloaks each embroidered with a huge yellow cross. They sat down on the rock, on the steps, on the ground at the foot of the tower. The last to arrive had white hair and he climbed up to the highest part of the wall. His figure was lit by the flames from the fires, and the wind caught his black cloak.

Almost everyone present knelt down and, bending forward, hands pressed together in prayer, beat their head three times on the ground. Talbo and his mercenaries remained standing. They had only been hired to fight.

'We have been granted surrender,' said the priest. 'You are all free to leave.'

A great sigh of relief came from the crowd.

'The souls belonging to the Other God will remain in the kingdom of this world. The souls belonging to the True God will return to his infinite mercy. The war will continue, but it is not an eternal war, because the Other God will be defeated in the end, even though some of the angels have already been corrupted by him. The Other God will be vanquished, but not destroyed; he will remain in hell for all eternity, along with the souls he managed to seduce.'

The people in the crowd stared at the man standing on the wall. They were not so sure now that they wanted to escape and thus suffer for all eternity.

'The Cathar Church is the true Church,' the priest went on. 'Thanks to Jesus Christ and to the Holy Spirit, we have achieved communion with God. We do not need to be reincarnated. We do not need to return to the kingdom of the Other God.'

Loni noticed that three priests bearing Bibles had stepped forward.

'The *consolamentum* will now be distributed to those who wish to die with us. Down below, the fire awaits. It will be a horrible death, involving terrible suffering. It will be a slow death, and the pain of the flames burning your flesh will be unlike any you have experienced before. However, not all of you will have that honour, only the true Cathars. The others will be condemned to live.'

Two women shyly went up to the priests who were holding the Bibles. An adolescent boy wrenched himself free from his mother's arms and joined them.

Four mercenaries approached Talbo.

'We want to receive the Sacrament, sir. We want to be baptised.'

'This is how the Tradition survives,' said the Voices. 'Because people are willing to die for an idea.'

Loni waited to hear Talbo's decision. The mercenaries had fought all their lives purely for money, until they met these people prepared to fight only for what they deemed to be right.

Talbo finally nodded his assent, even though it meant losing some of his best men.

'Let's go,' said Loni. 'Let's go over to the walls. They said that anyone who wants to can leave.'

'It's better that we rest, Loni.'

'You're going to die,' whispered the Voices again.

'I want to see the Pyrenees. I want to see the valley one more time, Talbo. You know that I'm going to die.'

Yes, he knew. He was a man accustomed to battlefields and he could tell when a wound would prove to be the death of one of his soldiers. Loni's wound had been open for three days, poisoning her blood. Those whose wounds did not heal might last two days or two weeks, but never longer than that.

And Loni was close to death. Her fever had passed. Talbo knew that this, too, was a bad sign. As long as the foot hurt and the fever burned, that meant the organism was still fighting. Now the struggle was over, and it was only a matter of time.

'You're not afraid,' said the Voices. No, Loni wasn't afraid. Even as a child, she had known that death was merely another beginning. At that time, the Voices had been her great companions. They had faces, bodies and gestures visible only to her. They were people who came from different worlds; they talked to her and never let her feel lonely. She'd had a very interesting childhood, playing with the other children, but using her invisible friends to shift objects around and make strange noises that startled her companions. Her mother was glad that they lived in a Cathar country – 'if the Catholics were here, you'd be burned alive,' she used to say. The Cathars paid no attention to such things; they believed that the good were good, the bad were bad, and that no force in the Universe could change this.

Then the French arrived, saying that there was no Cathar country, and, since the age of eight, all she had known was war.

The war had brought her one very good thing: her husband, hired in some distant land by the Cathar priests, who never themselves took up arms. But it brought something bad too: the fear of being burned alive, because the Catholics were moving ever closer to her village. She began to feel afraid of her invisible friends, and they gradually disappeared from her life. However, the Voices remained. They continued to tell her what was going to happen and how she should behave, but she didn't want their friendship, because they always knew too much. Then one Voice taught her the trick of thinking about that ancient tree, and she hadn't heard the Voices at all since the last crusade against the Cathars had begun, and the French Catholics had continued to win battle after battle.

Today, though, she didn't have the strength to think about the tree. The Voices were back, and she didn't mind. On the contrary, she needed them. They would show her the path once she was dead.

'Don't worry about me, Talbo. I'm not afraid of dying,' she said.

They reached the top of the wall. A cold, relentless wind was blowing, and Talbo drew his cloak more tightly about him. Loni didn't feel the cold any more. She could see the lights of a town on the horizon, and the lights of the encampment at the foot of the mountain. All along the valley bottom bonfires were lit. The French soldiers were awaiting the final decision.

The notes from a flute wafted up from below, along with the sound of voices singing.

'It's the soldiers,' said Talbo. 'They know they could die at any moment, and that's why, for them, life is one long celebration.'

Loni felt suddenly furious with life. The Voices were telling her that Talbo would meet other women, have children and grow rich on what he plundered from cities. 'But he will never love anyone as he has loved you, because you are part of him for ever,' said the Voices.

Loni and Talbo, their arms about each other, remained for a while gazing down on the landscape below, listening to the soldiers singing. Loni sensed that the mountain had been the setting of other wars in the past, a past so remote that not even the Voices could remember it.

'We are eternal, Talbo. That's what the Voices used to tell me in the days when I could see their bodies and faces.'

Talbo knew about his wife's Gift, but she had not mentioned it for a long time. Perhaps it was the effect of the fever.

'And yet no one life is the same as any other life. It might be that we will never meet again, and I need you to know that I've loved you all my life. I loved you even before I met you. You're part of me.

'I'm going to die, and since tomorrow is as good a day to die as any, I would like to die with the priests. I've never understood their ideas about the world, but they have always understood me. I want to accompany them into the next life. I might prove to be a good guide, because I've visited those worlds before.'

Loni thought how ironic fate was. She had been afraid of the Voices because they might set her on the path that would lead her to the fire, and yet there the fire was, waiting for her.

Talbo looked at his wife. Her eyes were growing dull, and yet she still retained the same peculiar charm that had first drawn him to her. He had never told her certain things, about the women he received as part of the booty of battle, the women he met while he was travelling the world, the women who were expecting him to return one day. He hadn't told her this because he was certain that she knew everything anyway and forgave him because he was her great love, and a great love is above the things of this world.

But there was something else he had never told her, and which she would possibly never know: that she, with her affection and her gaiety, had been largely responsible for him having rediscovered the meaning of life, that her love had driven him to the far corners of the Earth, because he needed to be rich enough to buy some land and live in peace with her for the rest of his days. It was his utter confidence in this fragile creature, whose life was now fading fast, that had made him fight with honour, because he knew that after the battle he could forget all the horrors of war in her arms, and that, despite all the women he had known, only there in her arms could he close his eyes and sleep like a child.

'Go and call the priest, Talbo,' she said. 'I want to be baptised.'

Talbo hesitated for a moment. Only warriors choose how they will die, but that woman had given her life for love, and perhaps, for her, love was a strange form of war.

He got up and walked down the steps in the wall. Loni tried to concentrate on the music coming from below and which was somehow making dying easier. Meanwhile, the Voices kept talking.

'In her life, every woman can make use of the Four Rings of Revelation. You have used only one, the wrong one,' they said.

Loni looked at her fingers. They were torn and cracked, the nails filthy. There was no ring. The Voices laughed.

'You know what we mean,' they said. 'The virgin, the saint, the martyr and the witch.'

Loni knew in her heart what the Voices were saying, but she couldn't remember what it meant. She had heard about it a long time ago, in an age when people dressed differently and saw the world differently too. She'd had another name then, and had spoken another language.

'They are the four ways in which a woman can commune with the Universe,' the Voices said, as if it were important for her to recall these ancient things. 'The Virgin has the power of both man and woman. She is condemned to Solitude, but Solitude reveals its secrets. That is the price paid by the Virgin – to need no one, to wear herself out in her love for others, and, through Solitude, to discover the wisdom of the world.'

Loni was still looking at the encampment down below. Yes, she knew these things.

'And the Martyr,' the Voices went on, 'the Martyr has the power of those who cannot be harmed by pain and suffering. She surrenders herself, suffers and, through Sacrifice, discovers the wisdom of the world.'

Loni again looked at her hands. There, shining invisibly, she saw the ring of the Martyr encircling one of her fingers.

'You could have chosen the revelation of the Saint, even if it wasn't the right ring for you,' the Voices said. 'The Saint has the courage of those for whom giving is the only way of receiving. They are a bottomless well from which people can constantly draw water to drink. And if the well runs dry, the Saint offers her blood so that others need never go thirsty. Through surrender, the Saint discovers the wisdom of the world.'

The Voices fell silent. Loni heard Talbo coming up the stone steps. She knew which ring should have been hers in that life, because it was the one she had worn in all her past lives, when she had been known by other names and had spoken other tongues. With that ring, the wisdom of the world was discovered through Pleasure, but she didn't want to think about that now. The ring of the Martyr was shining, invisible, on her finger.

Talbo came closer. And suddenly, when she gazed up at him, Loni noticed that the night had a magical glow to it, as if it were a sunny day.

'Wake up,' said the Voices.

But these were different voices, which she had never heard before. She felt someone rubbing her left wrist.

'Come on, Brida, get up.'

She opened her eyes and immediately closed them again, because the light from the sky was so intense. What a strange thing Death was.

'Open your eyes,' said Wicca.

But she needed to go back to the castle. A man she loved had gone off in search of a priest. She couldn't just run away. He was alone and he needed her.

'Tell me what your Gift is.'

Wicca didn't give her time to think. She knew she had been through something extraordinary, much more powerful than her experience with the tarot cards. Yet still she didn't give her time to think. She neither understood nor respected her feelings; all she wanted was to find out what her Gift was.

'Talk to me about your Gift,' Wicca insisted.

Brida took a deep breath, holding in her anger, but there was no escape. The woman would keep insisting until she told her what she wanted to know.

'I was a woman in love with ...'

Wicca quickly covered Brida's mouth. Then she stood up, made a few strange gestures in the air and turned back to her.

'God is the word. Always be very careful what you say in any situation and at any moment.'

Brida didn't understand why Wicca was behaving like this.

'God manifests himself in everything, but the word is one of his most favoured methods of doing so, because the word is thought transformed into vibration; you are projecting into the air around you something which, before, was only energy. Take great care with everything you say,' Wicca said again. 'The word has more power than many rituals.'

Brida still didn't understand. The only way she had of describing her experience was through words.

'When you spoke of a woman,' Wicca explained, 'you were not that woman. You were part of her. Other people might well have the same memory as you.'

Brida felt robbed. That woman had been so strong, and she didn't want to share her with anyone. Besides, there was Talbo too.

'Talk to me about your Gift,' Wicca said yet again. She couldn't allow the girl to be too dazzled by the experience. This form of time travel often brought problems.

'I have so many things to tell, and I need to talk to you, because no one else will believe me. Please,' begged Brida.

She began to tell her everything, from the moment when the rain was dripping on her face. She had a chance and she couldn't waste it, the chance to be with someone who believed in the extraordinary. She knew that no one else would listen to her with the same respect, because people were afraid of discovering that life was magical. They were used to their houses, their jobs, their expectations, and if someone turned up saying that it was possible to travel in time, that it was possible to see castles adrift in the Universe, tarot cards that told stories, men who walked through the dark night, people who had never experienced such things would feel that life had cheated them. Life, as far as they were concerned, was the same every day, every night, every weekend.

That's why Brida needed to seize that chance. If words were God, then let it be recorded on the air around her that she had travelled back in time and that she remembered every detail as if it were now, as if it were the wood where they were right now. And so, when, later on, someone managed to prove to her that none of this had happened, when time and space made her doubt it all, when she herself was convinced that it had been mere illusion, the words spoken that evening, there in the wood, would still be vibrating in the air and at least one person, someone for whom magic was part of life, would know that it had really happened.

She described the castle, the priests in the black and yellow robes, the valley filled with fires, the husband thinking thoughts that she could read without him speaking them. Wicca listened patiently, only showing any interest when she told her about the voices that appeared in Loni's mind. Then she would interrupt and ask if the voices were male or female (they were both), if they expressed any particular emotion, aggression or sympathy (no, they were impersonal), and if she could summon up the voices whenever she wished (she didn't know, she hadn't had time to find out).

'All right, we can leave now,' said Wicca, taking off her cloak and putting it back in her bag. Brida was disappointed. She thought she might receive some words of praise, or, at the very least, some explanation. But Wicca resembled one of those doctors who study their patient very coolly and objectively, more interested in noting down symptoms than in understanding the pain and suffering caused by those symptoms.

They made the long journey back. Whenever Brida tried to raise the subject again, Wicca would show a sudden interest in the increase in the cost of living, in the rush-hour traffic jams and the difficulties she was having with the manager of the building where she lived.

Only when they were once more sitting in the usual two armchairs did Wicca comment on Brida's experience.

'I just want to say one thing to you,' she said. 'Don't bother trying to explain your emotions. Live everything as intensely as you can and keep whatever you felt as a gift from God. If you think that you won't be able to stand a world in which living is more important than understanding, then give up magic now. The best way to destroy the bridge between the visible and the invisible is by trying to explain your emotions.'

Emotions were like wild horses, and Brida knew that reason could never entirely master them. Once, when a boyfriend left her, giving no explanation, she had stayed at home for months, going over and over his many defects and the thousand and one things that had been wrong with their relationship. Yet she woke up every morning thinking about him and knowing that if he phoned her, she would probably agree to meet.

The dog in the kitchen barked. Brida knew this was a sign that her visit was over.

'Oh, please, we haven't even talked about what happened!' she cried. 'And there are two questions I simply must ask.'

Wicca stood up. The girl always found a way of leaving any important questions to the very last moment, just when it was time for her to leave.

'I want to know if the priests I saw really existed.'

'We have extraordinary experiences and, less than two hours later, we're trying to convince ourselves that it was the mere product of our imagination,' said Wicca, going over to the bookshelves. Brida remembered that when they were in the wood, she herself had been thinking about people who were afraid of the extraordinary. And she felt ashamed of herself.

Wicca returned, bearing a book.

'The Cathars, or the Perfect Ones, were the priests of a church founded in the south of France at the end of the twelfth century. They believed in reincarnation and in the existence of absolute Good and absolute Evil. The world was divided into the chosen and the lost, which meant that there was no point in trying to convert anyone.

'The Cathars' indifference to worldly values led many of the feudal lords in the Languedoc region to adopt their religion as a way of avoiding having to pay the heavy taxes imposed at the time by the Catholic Church. Equally, since it had been decided at birth who was good and who was bad, the Cathars were very tolerant in their attitude to sex and, in particular, in their attitude to women. They were only strict about such matters with those who had been ordained as priests.

'Everything was fine until Catharism started to spread. The Catholic Church felt threatened and called for a crusade against the heretics. For forty years, Cathars and Catholics fought bloody battles, but the legalist forces, with the support of various other nations, finally managed to destroy all the towns that had adopted the new religion. Only the fortress of Monségur, in the Pyrenees, remained, and the Cathars besieged there held out until the French discovered the secret passageway through which they had been receiving supplies. One March morning in 1244, after the surrender of the castle, two hundred and twenty Cathars hurled themselves, singing, into the huge bonfire lit at the bottom of the mountain on which the castle had been built.'

Wicca said all this with the book, still closed, on her lap. Only when she had finished her story did she open it and leaf through it, looking for a photograph.

Brida saw the ruined building, with the tower almost completely destroyed, but with the walls intact. There was the courtyard, the steps Loni and Talbo had climbed, the rock that formed part of the wall and the tower.

'You said there was another question you wanted to ask me.'

The question was of no importance now. Brida could hardly think straight. She felt odd. With some effort she managed to remember what it was she had wanted to ask.

'I want to know why you're wasting your time with me, why you want to teach me.'

'Because that is what the Tradition is telling me to do,' replied Wicca. 'In your successive incarnations, you changed very little. You belong to the same group as people like myself and my friends. We are the ones charged with maintaining the Tradition of the Moon. You are a witch.'

Brida paid no attention to what Wicca was saying. It didn't even occur to her to make another appointment to meet. All she wanted at that moment was to leave, to be among ordinary things that would bring her back to her familiar world; a damp stain on the wall, a packet of cigarettes discarded on the floor, some letters left on the porter's desk.

'I have to work tomorrow.' She was suddenly concerned about the time.

On her way back home, she started pondering her company's invoicing system for exports and came up with a way of simplifying certain administrative procedures. She felt very pleased. Her boss might approve of what she was doing and, who knows, give her a raise.

She got home, had supper and watched a bit of television. Then she wrote down her thoughts about invoicing on a piece of paper and fell, exhausted, into bed.

The invoicing of exports had taken on great importance in her life. That, after all, was what she was paid to do.

Nothing else existed. Everything else was a lie.

For a whole week, Brida woke promptly, worked hard at the office and received due praise from her boss. She didn't miss one of her classes and took an interest in everything printed in all the magazines at the newsagent's. All she needed was to avoid thinking. Whenever thoughts surfaced of her meeting with a Magus in the forest or with a witch in the city, she immediately drove them out by reminding herself that she had exams next week or by recalling a remark made by one female friend about another.

Friday came around, and her boyfriend met her outside the university to go to the cinema. Afterwards, they went to their usual bar, talked about the film, their colleagues, and about their respective jobs. They bumped into friends who were on their way back from a party and decided to join them for supper, grateful that, in Dublin, you could always find a restaurant open.

At two o'clock in the morning, they said goodbye to their friends and decided to go back to her place. As soon as they got in, she put on a record by Iron Butterfly and poured them each a double whiskey. They lay on the sofa with their arms around each other, silent and abstracted, while he stroked her hair and her breasts.

'It's been a really crazy week,' she said suddenly. 'I worked non-stop, prepared for my exams and did all the shopping.'

The record finished. She got up to turn it over.

'You know the cupboard door in the kitchen, the one that had come unstuck? Well, I finally managed to arrange a date for someone to come and fix it. And I had to go to the bank several times as well, once to collect some money my Dad sent me, and again to deposit some cheques for the firm and then …'

Lorens was staring at her.

'Why are you staring at me?' she asked rather aggressively. Who was this man lying on the sofa, staring at her, incapable of saying anything of interest? It was quite absurd. She didn't need him. She didn't need anyone.

'Why are you staring at me?' she asked again.

But he said nothing. He merely stood up, went over to her and very tenderly led her back to the sofa.

'You're not listening to anything I say,' said Brida, confused.

Lorens put his arms around her.

'Emotions are like wild horses,' she thought.

'Tell me everything,' Lorens said sweetly. 'I'll listen and respect whatever decision you make, even if you've met someone else, even if this is goodbye. We've been together for a while now. I may not know you that well; I mean, I don't know exactly who you are, but I know who you're not. And you haven't been yourself all night.'

Brida felt like crying, but she'd shed so many tears already over dark nights, talking tarot cards and enchanted forests. Emotions really were like wild horses, and all she could do now was set them free.

She sat down in front of him, remembering that the Magus and Wicca both favoured that position. Then she gave him a complete account of everything that had happened since her meeting with the Magus in the forest. Lorens listened in total silence. When she told him about the photograph of Monségur, Lorens asked if she had perhaps heard about the Cathars in one of her university courses.

'Look, I know you don't believe a word of what I've told you,' she retorted. 'You think it was my unconscious mind, that I just remembered things I already knew, but no, Lorens, I had never heard of the Cathars before. But you, of course, have an explanation for everything.'

Her hands were shaking uncontrollably. Lorens got to his feet, picked up a piece of paper and made two holes in it, about eight inches apart. He placed the sheet of paper on the table, leaning it against the whiskey bottle, so that it was vertical.

Then he went into the kitchen and returned bearing a cork.

He sat at the head of the table, pushed the piece of paper and the bottle to the other end, and put the cork in front of him.

'Come over here,' he said.

Brida got up. She was trying to hide her shaking hands, not that he appeared to notice.

'Let's pretend that this cork is an electron, one of the small particles that make up the atom. Do you understand?'

She nodded.

'Right, well listen carefully. If I had certain highly complicated bits of apparatus with me that would allow me to shoot an electron in the direction of that piece of paper, it would pass through the two holes at the same time, except that it would do so without splitting into two.'

'I don't believe it,' she said. 'That's impossible.'

Lorens took the piece of paper and threw it away. Then, being a tidy person, he put the cork back where it belonged.

'You may not believe it, but it's true. It's something that scientists know but can't explain. I don't believe a thing you've told me, but I know that it's true.'

Brida's hands were still shaking, but she wasn't crying and she didn't lose control. All she noticed was that the effect of the alcohol had completely worn off. She was strangely lucid.

'And what do scientists do when confronted by these mysteries?'

'They enter the Dark Night, to use a term you taught me. We know that the mystery won't ever go away and so we learn to accept it, to live with it. I think the same thing happens in many situations in life. A mother bringing up a child must feel that she's plunging into the Dark Night too. Or an immigrant who travels to a far-off country in search of work and money. They believe that their efforts will be rewarded and that one day they'll understand what happened along the way which, at the time, seemed so very frightening. It isn't explanations that carry us forward, it's our desire to go on.'

Brida suddenly felt immensely tired. She needed to sleep. Sleep was the only magical kingdom into which she could freely enter.

That night, she had a beautiful dream full of seas and leafy islands. She woke in the early hours and was glad that Lorens was there beside her. She got up and went over to the bedroom window where she looked out over the sleeping city of Dublin.

She thought of her father who used to do just that whenever she woke feeling frightened. The memory brought with it another scene from her childhood.

She was on the beach with her father, and he asked her to go and see what the temperature of the water was like. She was five years old and glad to be able to help. She went to the water's edge and dipped in a toe.

'I put my feet in and it's cold,' she told him.

Her father picked her up and carried her down to the water again and, without any warning, threw her in. She was shocked at first, but then laughed out loud at the trick he'd played.

'How's the water?' asked her father.

'It's lovely,' she replied.

'Right, from now on, whenever you want to find out about something, plunge straight in.'

She had quickly forgotten this lesson. She may only have been twenty-one, but she had already nurtured many enthusiasms, which she had abandoned as quickly as she had taken them up. She wasn't afraid of difficulties; what frightened her was being forced to choose one particular path.

Choosing a path meant having to miss out on others. She had a whole life to live and she was always thinking that, in future, she might regret the choices she made now.

'I'm afraid of committing myself,' she thought to herself. She wanted to follow all possible paths and so ended up following none.

Even in that most important area of her life, love, she had failed to commit herself. After her first romantic disappointment, she had never again given herself entirely. She feared pain, loss and separation. These things were inevitable on the path to love, and the only way of avoiding them was by deciding not to take that path at all. In order not to suffer, you had to renounce love. It was like putting out your own eyes in order not to see the bad things in life.

'Life is so complicated.'

You had to take risks, follow some paths and abandon others. She remembered Wicca telling her about people who followed certain paths only to prove that they weren't the right ones, but that wasn't as bad as choosing a path and then spending the rest of your life wondering if you'd made the right choice. No one could make a choice without feeling afraid.

That was the law of life. That was the Dark Night, and no one could escape the Dark Night, even if they never made a decision, even if they lacked the courage to change anything, because that in itself was a decision, a change, except without the benefit of the treasures hidden in the Dark Night.

Lorens might be right. In the end, they would laugh at their initial fears. Just as she had laughed at the snakes and scorpions she had imagined were there in the forest. In her despair, she had forgotten that Ireland's patron saint, St Patrick, had long ago driven out all the snakes.

'I'm so glad you exist, Lorens,' she said softly, afraid that he might hear.

She went back to bed and soon fell asleep. Before she did, though, she remembered another story about her father. It was Sunday, and they and all the family were having lunch at her grandmother's house. She must have been about fourteen, and she was complaining about not being able to do a piece of homework, because every time she started, it went wrong.

'Perhaps the times when it goes wrong are teaching you something,' said her father. But Brida was sure that she'd taken the wrong path and that there was no way to put things right.

Her father took her by the hand and led her into the living room, where her grandmother used to watch television. There was a large, antique grandfather clock, which had stopped years before because it could no longer be repaired.

'Nothing in the world is ever completely wrong, my dear,' said her father, looking at the clock. 'Even a stopped clock is right twice a day.'

She walked for some time in the wooded mountains before she found the Magus. He was sitting on a rock, near the top of the mountain, contemplating the valley and the mountains to the west. It was a really beautiful view, and Brida recalled that spirits preferred such places.

'Is God only the God of beauty?' she asked as she approached. 'If so, what about the ugly people and places of the world?'

The Magus did not reply. Brida felt embarrassed.

'You probably don't remember me. I was here two months ago. I spent the whole night alone in the forest. I promised myself that I would only come back when I had discovered my path. I've met a woman called Wicca.'

The Magus started, but realised with relief that the girl hadn't noticed. Then he smiled to himself at the irony of fate.

'Wicca told me that I'm a witch,' the girl went on.

'Don't you trust her?'

This was the first question the Magus had asked since she arrived, and Brida was pleased to know that he was actually listening to what she was saying. Up until then, she hadn't been sure.

'Yes, I trust her,' she said. 'And I trust in the Tradition of the Moon. But I know, too, that the Tradition of the Sun helped me by forcing me to understand about the Dark Night. That's why I came back.'

'Then sit down and enjoy the sunset,' said the Magus.

'I'm not staying alone in the forest again,' she replied. 'The last time I was here ...'

The Magus interrupted her:

'Don't say that. God is in the word.'

Wicca had said much the same thing.

'What did I say wrong?'

'If you say it was the "last" time, it might well turn out to be the last. What you meant was "the most recent time I was here".'

Brida was worried. She would have to take great care with her words from now on. She decided to sit quietly and do as the Magus said and watch the sunset.

Doing so made her nervous. It would not be dark for nearly an hour, and she had a lot to talk about and many things to say and ask. Whenever she sat still, just looking at something, she got the feeling that she was wasting precious time when she should be doing things or meeting people. She could be spending her time so much better, because there was still so much to learn. And yet, as the sun sank lower on the horizon, and the clouds filled up with rays of gold and pink, Brida had the feeling that what she was struggling for in life was exactly this, to be able to sit one day and contemplate just such a sunset.

'Do you know how to pray?' asked the Magus at one point.

Of course she did. Everyone knew how to pray.

'Right, as soon as the sun touches the horizon, say a prayer. In the Tradition of the Sun, it is through prayers that we commune with God. A prayer, when couched in the words of the soul, is far more powerful than any ritual.'

'I don't know how to pray, because my soul is silent,' said Brida.

The Magus laughed.

'Only the truly enlightened have silent souls.'

'So why can't I pray with my soul, then?'

'Because you lack the humility to listen to it and find out what it wants. You're embarrassed to listen to the urgings of your soul and afraid to take those requests to God, because you think he doesn't have time to concern himself with them.'

She was watching a sunset, sitting beside a sage. However, as always happened at such moments, she had the feeling that she didn't deserve to be there.

'It's true that I feel unworthy. I always think the spiritual search was made for people better than me.'

'Those people, if they exist, don't need to search for anything. They are the manifestation of the spirit. The search was made for people like us.'

'Like us,' he had said, and yet he was a long way ahead of her.

'God is God in both the Tradition of the Moon and the Tradition of the Sun,' said Brida, believing that the Traditions were the same and only differed in the ways in which they were taught. 'So teach me how to pray.'

The Magus turned to face the sun and closed his eyes.

'We are human beings, Lord, and we do not know our own greatness. Lord, give us the humility to ask for what we need, because no desire is vain and no request is futile. Each of us knows how best to feed our own soul; give us the courage to see our desires as coming from the fount of Your eternal Wisdom. Only by accepting our desires can we begin to understand who we are. Amen. Now it's your turn,' said the Magus.

'Lord, help me understand that all the good things in life that happen to me do so because I deserve them. Help me understand that what moves me to seek out Your truth is the same force that moved the saints, and the doubts I have are the same doubts that the saints had, and my frailties are the same frailties. Help me to be humble enough to accept that I am no different from other people. Amen.'

They sat in silence, watching the sunset, until the last ray of sun left the clouds. Their souls were praying, asking for wishes to be granted and giving thanks that they were together.

'Let's go to the pub,' said the Magus.

Brida and the Magus began the walk back. Again she remembered the day when she had first gone there in search of him. She promised herself that she would go over this story only one more time; she didn't need to keep trying to convince herself.

The Magus studied the girl walking ahead of him and trying to look as if she knew where she was putting her feet amongst the damp earth and the stones, but stumbling repeatedly. His heart grew lighter for a moment, then immediately grew guarded again.

Sometimes, certain of God's blessings arrive by shattering all the windows.

It was so good to have Brida by his side, thought the Magus, as they walked back down the mountain. He was just like other men, with the same frailties and the same virtues, and he still wasn't used to the role of Teacher. At first, when people used to come to that forest from all over Ireland to hear his teachings, he spoke of the Tradition of the Sun and asked people to understand what lay around them. God had stored His wisdom there and they were all capable of understanding it by performing a few simple rituals. The way of teaching the Tradition of the Sun had been described two thousand years before by the Apostle Paul: 'And I was with you in weakness and in much fear and trembling; and my speech and my message were not in plausible words of wisdom, but in demonstration of the Spirit and of power, that your faith might not rest in the wisdom of men but in the power of God.'

Yet people seemed incapable of understanding him when he talked to them about the Tradition of the Sun and were disappointed because he was a man just like other men.

He said it didn't matter; he was a Teacher, and all he was doing was giving each person the necessary means to acquire Knowledge. But they needed much more; they needed a guide. They didn't understand about the Dark Night; they didn't understand that any guide through the Dark Night would only illuminate, with his torch, what he himself wanted to see. And if, by chance, that torch should go out, the people would be lost, because they didn't know the way back. But they needed a guide, and to be a good Teacher, he, too, had to accept the needs of others.

So he started padding out his teachings with unnecessary but fascinating things that everyone could accept and understand. The method worked. People learned the Tradition of the Sun, and when they finally realised that many of the things the Magus had told them to do were absolutely useless, they laughed at themselves. And the Magus was glad, because he had finally learned how to teach.

Brida was different. Her prayer had deeply touched the Magus's soul. She had understood that no human being who has walked this planet was or is different from the others. Few people were capable of saying out loud that the great Teachers from the past had the same qualities and the same defects as all men, and that this in no way diminished their ability to search for God. Judging oneself to be inferior to other people was one of the worst acts of pride he knew, because it was the most destructive way of being different.

* * *

When they reached the bar, the Magus ordered two whiskies.

'Look at the other customers,' Brida said. 'They probably come here every night. They probably always do the same thing.'

The Magus was suddenly not so sure that Brida really did consider herself to be the same as everyone else.

'You concern yourself too much with other people,' he replied. 'They're a mirror of yourself.'

'Yes, I know. I thought I knew what made me happy and what made me sad, then suddenly I realised that I need to think again. But it's very hard.'

'What made you change your mind?'

'Love. I know a man who makes me feel complete. Three days ago, he showed me that his world is full of mysteries too and that I'm not alone.'

The Magus remained impassive, but he was remembering the thought he'd had earlier about God's blessings sometimes shattering windows.

'Do you love him?'

'What I've realised is that I could love him still more. Even if I learn nothing new on this path, at least I will have learned one important thing: we have to take risks.'

He had been making great plans for that night as they walked down the mountain. He wanted to show how much he needed her, to show that he was just like other men, weary of so much solitude. But all she wanted were answers to her questions.

'There's something strange about the air here,' Brida said. The atmosphere appeared to have changed.

'It's the Messengers,' said the Magus. 'Artificial demons, those who do not form part of God's Left Arm, those who do not lead us to the light.'

His eyes were shining. Something really had changed, and there he was talking about demons.

'God created the legion of His Left Arm in order to improve us, so that we would know what to do with our mission,' he went on. 'But He put man in charge of concentrating the powers of darkness and creating his own demons.'

And that was what he was doing now.

'But we can concentrate the forces of good too,' said the girl, somewhat alarmed.

'No, we can't.'

He needed to be distracted, if only she would ask him something. He didn't want to create a demon. In the Tradition of the Sun, they were called Messengers, and they could do great good or great evil – only the most important Teachers were allowed to invoke them. He was one of those Teachers, but he didn't want to invoke such a Messenger now, because a Messenger could be a dangerous force, especially when mixed up with disappointments in love.

Brida was confused by his response. The Magus was behaving strangely.

'We can't concentrate the Forces of Good,' he said again, trying hard to focus on what he was saying. 'The Force for Good is always diffused, like Light. When you give off positive vibrations, you benefit all humankind, but when you concentrate the force of the Messenger, you are only benefiting – or harming – yourself.'

His eyes were still shining. He called over the landlord and paid the bill.

'Let's go to my place,' he said. 'I'm going to make some tea and you can tell me about the really important questions in your life.'

Brida hesitated. He was an attractive man, and she was an attractive woman. That night, she feared, might put an end to her apprenticeship.

'I must take risks,' she said to herself again.

The Magus lived a little way outside the village. Brida noticed that although his house was very different from Wicca's, it was equally comfortable and just as tastefully decorated. However, there wasn't a book in sight; it was mainly empty space and a few bits of furniture.

They went into the kitchen to make tea, then came back to the living room.

'Why did you come here today?' asked the Magus.

'I promised myself that I would, once I knew something.'

'And what do you know?'

'Well, I know a little. I know that the path is simple and therefore more difficult than I thought. But I will simplify my soul. Anyway, my first question is: "Why are you wasting your time with me?"'

'Because you're my Soulmate,' thought the Magus, but he said:

'Because I need someone to talk to.'

'What do you think of the path I've chosen – the Tradition of the Moon?'

The Magus needed to tell the truth, even though he wished the truth was different.

'It was your path. Wicca is quite right. You are a witch. You will learn to use Time's memory to discover the lessons that God taught.'

And he wondered why life was like this, why he had met his Soulmate only to find that the one way she could learn was through the Tradition of the Moon.

'I only have one more question,' said Brida. It was getting late; soon there would be no more buses. 'I need to know the answer, and I know that Wicca won't teach it to me. I know this because she's a woman like me. She'll always be my Teacher, but on this topic, she'll always be a woman. I want to know how to find my Soulmate.'

'He's right here with you,' thought the Magus, but again said nothing. He went over to one corner of the room and turned out the lights. Only a kind of acrylic sculpture remained lit. Brida hadn't noticed when she came in. It contained some sort of liquid, and bubbles rose and fell inside it, filling the room with red and blue lights.

'We've met twice now,' said the Magus, his eyes fixed on the sculpture. 'I only have permission to teach through the Tradition of the Sun. The Tradition of the Sun awakens in people the ancestral knowledge that they possess.'

'How do I find my Soulmate through the Tradition of the Sun?'

'That's what everyone here on Earth is searching for,' the Magus said, unwittingly echoing Wicca's words. 'Perhaps they'd been taught by the same Teacher,' Brida thought.

'And the Tradition of the Sun placed in the world, for everyone to see, the sign that someone is their Soulmate: a particular light in the eye.'

'I've seen lots of different kinds of light in lots of people's eyes,' Brida said. 'Today, for example, I saw your eyes shining. That's what everyone looks for.'

'She's forgotten her prayer,' thought the Magus. 'She thinks she's different from everyone else. She's incapable of recognising what God is generous enough to show her.'

'I don't understand eyes,' she insisted. 'Tell me instead how people discover their Soulmate through the Tradition of the Moon.'

The Magus turned to her, his eyes cold and expressionless.

'You're sad,' she said, 'and you're sad because I'm still incapable of learning through the simple things. What you don't understand is that people suffer, they search and search for love, not knowing that they're fulfilling the divine mission of finding their Soulmate. You forget – because you're a wise man and don't think about what it's like for ordinary people – that I carry millennia of disappointment within me, and I can no longer learn certain things through the simple things of life.'

The Magus remained impassive.

'A point of light,' he said. 'A point of light above the left shoulder of your Soulmate. That is how it is in the Tradition of the Moon.'

'I have to leave,' she said, hoping that he would ask her to stay. She liked being there. He had answered her question.

The Magus, however, got up and accompanied her to the door.

'I'm going to learn everything that you know,' she said. 'I'm going to discover how to see that point of light.'

The Magus waited until Brida had gone down the stairs. There was a bus to Dublin in the next half hour, so there was no need for him to worry about her. Then he went out into the garden and performed the ritual he performed every night. He was used to doing it, but sometimes he found it hard to achieve the necessary concentration. Tonight he was particularly distracted.

When the ritual was over, he sat down on the doorstep and looked up at the sky. He thought about Brida. He could see her on the bus, with the point of light above her left shoulder and which, because she was his Soulmate, only he could see. He thought how eager she must be to conclude a search that had started the day she was born. He thought how cold and distant she had been when they arrived at his house, and that this was a good sign. It meant she was confused about her own feelings. She was defending herself from something she couldn't understand.

He thought too, somewhat fearfully, that she was in love.

'Everyone finds their Soulmate, Brida,' he said out loud to the plants in his garden, but deep down, he sensed that he, too, despite all his years in the Tradition, still needed to reinforce his faith, and that he was really talking to himself.

'At some point in our lives, we all meet our Soulmate and recognise him or her,' he went on. 'If I were not a Magus and couldn't see the point of light above your left shoulder, it would take a little longer for me to accept you, but you would fight for me, and one day I would see the special light in your eyes. However, the fact is I *am* a Magus, and it's up to me to fight for you, so that all my knowledge is transformed into wisdom.'

He sat for a long time contemplating the night and thinking about Brida travelling back to Dublin on the bus. It was colder than usual. Summer would soon be over.

'There are no risks in Love, as you'll find out for yourself. People have been searching for and finding each other for thousands of years.'

Suddenly, he realised that he might be wrong. There was always a risk, a single risk: that one person might meet with more than one Soulmate in the same incarnation, as had happened millennia before.

Winter and Spring

Over the next two months, Wicca initiated Brida into the first mysteries of witchcraft. According to her, women could learn these things more quickly than men, because each month, they experienced in their own bodies the complete cycle of nature: birth, life and death, the 'Cycle of the Moon' as she called it.

Brida had to buy a new notebook and record in it any psychical experiences she'd had since her first meeting with Wicca. The notebook always had to be kept up to date and must bear on its cover a five-pointed star, which associated everything written in it with the Tradition of the Moon. Wicca told her that all witches owned such a book, known as a Book of Shadows, in homage to their sisters who had died during the four hundred years that the witch-hunt lasted.

'Why do I need to do all this?'

'We have to awaken the Gift. Without it, you will know only the Minor Mysteries. The Gift is your way of serving the world.'

Brida had to reserve one relatively unused corner of her house for a kind of miniature oratory in which a candle should be kept burning day and night. The candle, according to the Tradition of the Moon, was the symbol of the four elements, and contained within itself the earth of the wick, the water of the paraffin, the fire that burned and the air that allowed the fire to burn. The candle was also important as a way of reminding her that she had a mission to fulfil and that she was engaged on that mission. Only the candle should be visible; everything else should be hidden away on a shelf or in a drawer. From the Middle Ages on, the Tradition of the Moon had demanded that witches surround their activities with absolute secrecy, for there were several prophecies warning that Darkness would return at the end of the millennium.

Whenever Brida came home and saw the candle flame, she felt a strange, almost sacred, responsibility.

Wicca told her that she must always pay attention to the sound of the world. 'You can hear it wherever you are,' she said. 'It's a noise that never stops, which is there on mountain tops, in cities, in the sky and at the bottom of the ocean. This noise – which is like a vibration – is the Soul of the World transforming itself and travelling towards the light. Any witch must be keenly aware of this, because she is an important part of that journey.'

Wicca also explained that the Ancients spoke to our world through symbols. Even if no one was listening, even if the language of symbols had been forgotten by almost everyone, the Ancients never ceased talking.

'Are they beings like us?' Brida asked one day.

'We are them. And suddenly we understand everything that we learned in our past lives, and everything that the great sages left written on the Universe. Jesus said: "The Kingdom of God is as if a man should scatter seed upon the ground and should sleep and rise night and day, and the seed should sprout and grow, he knows not how."

'The human race drinks always from this same inexhaustible fountain, and even when everyone says it is doomed, it still finds a way to survive. It survived when the apes drove the men from the trees and when the waters covered the Earth. It will survive when everyone is preparing for the final catastrophe.

'We are responsible for the Universe, because we are the Universe.'

The more time Brida spent with Wicca, the more aware she became of what a very pretty woman she was.

icca continued to teach Brida the Tradition of the Moon. She told her to find a two-edged dagger with an undulating blade like a flame. Brida tried in various shops, but there was nothing suitable. In the end, Lorens solved the problem by asking a metallurgical chemistry engineer, who worked at the university, to make such a blade. Then he himself carved a wooden handle and gave the dagger to Brida as a gift. It was his way of saying that he respected her search.

The dagger was consecrated by Wicca in a complicated ritual involving magical words, charcoal designs drawn on the blade, and a few blows with a wooden spoon. The dagger was to be used as a prolongation of her own arm, keeping the energy of her body concentrated in the blade. Fairy godmothers used a wand for the same purpose, and magi used a sword.

When Brida expressed her surprise at the charcoal and the wooden spoon, Wicca said that, in the days of witch-hunts, witches were forced to use materials that could be mistaken for ordinary everyday objects. The tradition of the dagger, the charcoal and the wooden spoon had survived, while the actual materials once used by the Ancients had been lost entirely.

Brida learned how to burn incense and how to use the dagger inside magic circles. There was a ritual she had to perform whenever the moon changed its phase; she would place a cup of water on the windowsill so that the moon was reflected in the surface. Then she would stand so that her own face was reflected in the water and the moon's reflection was right in the middle of her forehead. When she was completely focused, she would cut the water with the dagger, causing the reflections to break up and form smaller ones.

This water had to be drunk immediately, and then the power of the moon would grow inside her.

'None of this makes sense,' Brida said once. Wicca ignored the remark, for she had once thought exactly the same, but she remembered Jesus' words about the things that grow inside each of us without our understanding how or why.

'It doesn't matter if it makes sense or not,' she told her. 'Think of the Dark Night. The more you do this, the more the Ancients will communicate with you. They will do so initially in ways you cannot understand, because only your soul will be listening, but one day, the voices will be heard again.'

Brida didn't want to hear voices, she wanted to find her Soulmate, but she said nothing of this to Wicca.

She was forbidden from returning to the past again. According to Wicca, this was rarely necessary.

'Don't use the cards to read the future either. The cards are to be used only for growth without words, the kind of growth that occurs imperceptibly.'

Brida had to spread the cards out on a table three times a week and sit looking at them. Occasionally she had visions, but they were usually incomprehensible. When she complained about this, Wicca said that the visions had a meaning so deep that she was incapable of understanding it.

'And why shouldn't I use the cards to read the future?'

'Only the present has power over our lives,' replied Wicca. 'When you read the future in the cards, you are bringing the future into the present, and that can cause serious harm. The present could confuse your future.'

Once a week, they went to the wood, and Wicca taught her apprentice the secrets of herbs. For Wicca, everything in the world bore God's signature, especially plants. Certain leaves resembled the heart and were good for heart disease, while flowers that resembled eyes could cure diseases of the eye. Brida began to understand that many herbs really did bear a close resemblance to human organs, and in a book on folk medicine that Lorens borrowed from the university library she found research indicating that the beliefs of country people and witches could well be right.

'God placed his pharmacy in the woods and fields,' Wicca said one day when they were resting under a tree, 'so that everyone could enjoy good health.'

Brida knew that her teacher had other apprentices, but she never met them – the dog always barked when her time with Wicca was up. However, she had passed other people on the stairs: an older woman, a girl about her own age and a man in a suit. Brida listened discreetly to their steps until the creaking floorboards above betrayed their destination: Wicca's apartment.

One day, Brida risked asking about these other students.

'Witchcraft is based on collective strength,' Wicca told her. 'All the different gifts keep the energy of our work in constant movement. Each gift depends on all the others.'

Wicca explained that there were nine gifts, and that both the Tradition of the Sun and the Tradition of the Moon took care that these gifts survived over the centuries.

'What are the nine gifts?'

Wicca told her off for being lazy and asking questions all the time, when a true witch should be interested in all forms of spiritual enquiry. Brida, she said, ought to spend more time reading the Bible ('which contains all the true occult wisdom') and to seek out the gifts in St Paul's First Epistle to the Corinthians. Brida did so and there she found the nine gifts: the word of wisdom, the word of knowledge, faith, healing, the working of miracles, prophecy, the discerning of the spirits, speaking in tongues and the interpretation of tongues.

It was only then that she understood the gift she was seeking: the discerning of the spirits.

Wicca taught Brida to dance. She said that she needed to learn to move her body in accordance with the sound of the world, that ever-present vibration. There was no special technique; it was simply a matter of making any movement that came into her head. Nevertheless, it took a while before Brida could become used to moving and dancing in that illogical way.

'The Magus of Folk taught you about the Dark Night. In both Traditions – which are, in fact, one – the Dark Night is the only way to grow. When you set off along the path of magic, the first thing you do is surrender yourself to a greater power, for you will encounter things that you will never understand.

'Nothing will behave in the logical way you have come to expect. You will understand things only with your heart, and that can be a little frightening. For a long time, the journey will seem like a Dark Night, but then any search is an act of faith.

'But God, who is far harder to understand than a Dark Night, appreciates our act of faith, and takes our hand and guides us through the Mystery.'

Wicca spoke of the Magus with no rancour or bitterness. Brida had been wrong; Wicca had clearly never had an affair with him; it was written in her eyes. Perhaps the irritation she had expressed on that first day had merely been because they had ended up following different paths. Wizards and witches were vain creatures, and each wanted to prove to the other that their path was the best.

She suddenly realised what she had thought.

She could tell Wicca wasn't in love with the Magus by her eyes.

She had seen films and read books that talked about this. The whole world could tell from someone's eyes if they were in love.

'I only manage to understand the simple things once I've embraced the complicated things,' she thought to herself. Perhaps one day she *would* follow the Tradition of the Sun.

It was quite late on in the year and the cold was just beginning to bite when Brida received a phone call from Wicca.

'We're going to meet in the wood in two days' time, on the night of the new moon, just before dark,' was all she said.

Brida spent those two days thinking about that meeting. She performed the usual rituals and danced to the sound of the world. 'I wish I could dance to some music,' she thought, but she was becoming used to moving her body according to that strange vibration, which she could hear better at night or in certain silent places. Wicca had told her that, when she danced to the sound of the world, her soul would feel more comfortable in her body and there would be a lessening of tension. Brida began to notice how people walking down the street didn't seem to know what to do with their hands or how to move their hips or shoulders. She felt like telling them that the world was playing a tune and if they danced a little to that music, and simply allowed their body to move illogically for a few minutes a day, they would feel much better.

That dance, however, was part of the Tradition of the Moon, and only witches knew about it. There must be something similar in the Tradition of the Sun. There always was, although no one appeared to want to learn it.

'We've lost our ability to live with the secrets of the world,' she said to Lorens. 'And yet there they are before us. The reason I want to be a witch is so that I can see those secrets.'

On the appointed day, Brida went to the wood. She walked amongst the trees, feeling the magical presence of the spirits of nature. About fifteen hundred years ago, that wood had been the sacred place of the Druids, until St Patrick drove the snakes from Ireland, and the Druid cults disappeared. Nevertheless, respect for that place had passed from generation to generation and, even now, the villagers both respected and feared it.

She found Wicca in the clearing, wrapped in her cloak. There were four other people with her, all wearing ordinary clothes and all of them women. In the place where she had once noticed ashes, a fire was burning. Brida looked at the fire and for some reason felt afraid. She didn't know if it was because of that part of Loni which she carried inside her or because she had known fire in her other incarnations.

More women arrived. Some were her age and others were older than Wicca. Altogether, there were nine.

'I didn't invite the men today. We are here waiting for the kingdom of the Moon.'

The kingdom of the Moon was the night.

They stood around the fire, talking about the most trivial things in the world, and Brida felt as if she'd been invited to a tea-party with a lot of old gossips, although the setting was rather different.

However, as soon as the sky filled up with stars, the atmosphere changed completely. Wicca didn't need to call for silence; gradually, the conversation died, and Brida wondered to herself if they'd only just noticed the presence of the fire and the forest.

After a brief silence, Wicca spoke.

'On this night, once a year, the world's witches gather together to pray and pay homage to our forebears. According to the Tradition, on the tenth moon of the year, we gather round a fire, which was life and death to our persecuted sisters.'

Brida produced a wooden spoon from beneath her cloak.

'Here is the symbol,' she said, showing the spoon to everyone.

The women remained standing and held hands. Then, raising their joined hands, they heard Wicca's prayer.

'May the blessing of the Virgin Mary and of her son Jesus be upon our heads tonight. In our bodies sleeps the Soulmate of our ancestors. May the Virgin Mary bless them.

'May she bless us because we are women and live in a world in which men love and understand us more and more. Yet still we bear on our bodies the marks of past lives, and those marks still hurt.

'May the Virgin Mary free us from those marks and put an end for ever to our sense of guilt. We feel guilty when we go out to work because we're leaving our children in order to earn money to feed them. We feel guilty when we stay at home because it seems we're not making the most of our freedom. We feel guilty about everything, because we have always been kept far from decision-making and from power.

'May the Virgin Mary remind us always that it was the women who stayed with Jesus when all the men fled and denied their faith. That it was the women who wept while he carried the cross and who waited at his feet at the hour of his death. That it was the women who visited the empty tomb, and that we have no reason to feel guilty.

'May the Virgin Mary remind us always that we were burned and persecuted because we preached the Religion of Love. When others were trying to stop time with the power of sin, we gathered together to hold forbidden festivals in which we celebrated what was still beautiful in the world. Because of this we were condemned and burned in the public squares.

'May the Virgin Mary remind us always that, while men were tried in the public square over land disputes, women were tried in the public square for adultery.

'May the Virgin Mary remind us always of our ancestors, who – like St Joan of Arc – had to disguise themselves as men in order to fulfil the Lord's word, and yet still they died in the fire.'

Wicca held the wooden spoon in both hands and stretched out both arms.

'Here is the symbol of our ancestors' martyrdom. May the flame that devoured their bodies remain always alight in our souls. Because they are in us. Because we are them.'

And she threw the spoon into the fire.

*B*rida continued to perform the rituals that Wicca had taught her. She kept the candle always burning and danced to the sound of the world. She noted down her meetings with Wicca in the *Book of Shadows* and went to the sacred wood twice a week. She noticed, to her surprise, that she was beginning to understand more about herbs and plants.

However, the voices that Wicca wanted to awaken did not appear. Nor did she manage to see the point of light above anyone's left shoulder.

'Who knows, perhaps I haven't yet met my Soulmate,' she thought rather fearfully. This was the fate of those who knew the Tradition of the Moon: never to make a mistake when choosing the man in their life. This meant that, from the moment they became a true witch, they would never again nurse the same illusions about love that other people did. True, this would mean less suffering or even no suffering at all, because they could love everything more intensely; finding one's Soulmate was, after all, a divine mission in everyone's life. Even if, one day, you were forced to part, love for your Soulmate – according to both Traditions – would always be crowned with glory, understanding and a kind of purifying nostalgia.

It meant, too, that, from the moment you became able to see the point of light, there would be no Dark Night of Love. Brida thought of the many times she had suffered for love, the nights she had lain awake waiting for a phone call that never came, the romantic weekends that didn't survive the following week, the parties spent glancing anxiously around to see who was there, the joy of making a conquest simply to prove that you could, the sadness and loneliness when you were sure that your best friend's boyfriend was the only man who could possibly make you happy. That was part of her world, and the world of everyone else she knew. That was love, and that was how people had searched for their Soulmate since time began, by looking into another person's eyes in search of that special light, desire. She had never given much value to such things; on the contrary, she had always thought it pointless to suffer because of someone else, or to feel scared stiff because you couldn't find anyone with whom to share your life. Now, however, that she had the chance to free herself from such fears for ever, she wasn't sure she wanted to.

'Do I really want to be able to see that point of light?'

She thought of the Magus – she was beginning to think he was right and that the Tradition of the Sun was the only way to deal with Love. But she couldn't change her mind now; she knew the path to follow, and she must follow it to the end. She knew that if she gave up now, she would find it harder and harder to make any choices in life.

* * *

One afternoon, after a long lesson devoted to rain-making rituals performed by the witches of old – rituals that Brida would have to note down in her *Book of Shadows* even though she would probably never use them – Wicca asked if she wore all the clothes she owned.

'No, of course I don't,' came the reply.

'Well, from now on, wear everything in your wardrobe.'

Brida thought perhaps she had misunderstood.

'Everything that contains our energy should be in constant movement,' Wicca explained. 'The clothes you bought are part of you, and they represent those special times when you left the house wanting to splash out a little because you were happy with the world, times when you'd been hurt and wanted to make yourself feel better or times when you thought you should change your life.

'Clothes always transform emotion into matter. It's one of the bridges between the visible and the invisible. Some clothes can even be harmful because they were made for someone else, but have ended up in your hands.'

Brida knew what she meant. There were some clothes she couldn't bring herself to wear, because whenever she did, something bad happened.

'Get rid of any clothes that were not intended for you,' Wicca went on. 'And wear all the others. It's important to keep the soil turned, the waves crashing and all your emotions in movement. The whole Universe is moving all the time, and we must do likewise.'

When she got home, Brida spread out the contents of her wardrobe on the bed. She looked at each item of clothing; there were some she'd completely forgotten about; others brought back happy memories, but were no longer fashionable. Brida kept them, though, because they held a special charm, and if she got rid of them, she might be undoing all the good things she had experienced while wearing them.

She looked at the clothes which she felt contained 'bad vibrations'. She'd always hoped that those bad vibrations might one day become good vibrations and then she would be able to wear the clothes again. However, whenever she put them to the test, the results were invariably disastrous.

She realised that her relationship with clothes was more complicated than she had thought, and yet it was hard to accept Wicca meddling in something as private and personal as the way she dressed. Some clothes had to be kept for special occasions, and only she could say when she should wear them. Others weren't suitable for work or even for going out at the weekend. Why was Wicca so interested in this? She never questioned what Wicca told her to do; she spent her life dancing and lighting candles, plunging knives into water and learning about rituals she would never use. And she accepted all that because it was part of the Tradition, a Tradition she didn't understand, but which was perhaps in touch with her unknown self. But by meddling with her clothes, Wicca was also meddling with her way of being in the world.

Perhaps Wicca had overstepped the bounds of her power. Perhaps she was trying to interfere in things she shouldn't.

'What is outside is harder to change than what is inside.'

Someone had said something. Brida instinctively looked around her, knowing that she would find no one.

It was the Voice.

The Voice that Wicca had wanted to awaken.

She managed to curb her feelings of excitement and fear. She remained silent, hoping to hear something else, but there was only the noise from the street, a television some way off and the omnipresent sound of the world. She tried to sit in the same position as before, to think the same things as before. Everything had happened so fast that she hadn't even felt frightened or surprised or proud.

But the Voice had said something. Even if everyone in the world were to prove to her that it was all just a product of her imagination, even if the witch-hunts were to return and she had to stand up in court and risked being burned to death, she was utterly sure that she'd heard a voice that was not her own.

'What is outside is more difficult to change than what is inside.' The Voice could perhaps have said something a little more earth shattering, given that this was the first time in her current incarnation that she was hearing it, but suddenly Brida was filled by an intense feeling of joy. She wanted to phone Lorens, to go and see the Magus, to tell Wicca that her Gift had finally been revealed, and that she could now become part of the Tradition of the Moon. She paced the room, smoked a few cigarettes, and only half an hour later did she feel calm enough to sit down again on the bed, along with all her clothes.

The Voice was right. Brida had surrendered her soul to a strange woman and – odd though it might seem – it was far easier to surrender her soul than her way of dressing.

Only now was she beginning to understand how much those apparently meaningless exercises were influencing her life. Only now, when she was considering changing on the outside, could she realise how much she had changed inside.

When they met again, Wicca wanted to know all about the Voice, and was pleased that Brida had noted down every detail in her *Book of Shadows*.

'Whose Voice is it?' asked Brida.

Wicca, however, had more important things to do and say than answer Brida's eternal questions.

'So far, I've shown you how to return to the path that your soul travelled several incarnations ago. I awoke that knowledge by speaking directly to it – with my soul – through the symbols and rituals of our forebears. You might have grumbled a bit about it, but your soul was glad because it was re-establishing contact with its mission. While you were getting irritated with all the exercises you had to do, feeling bored with the dancing and having to fight off sleep during rituals, your hidden side was once more drinking in the wisdom of Time, remembering what it had learned before, and as it says in the Bible, the seed was growing and sprouting, although you knew not how. Then came the moment to start to learn new things. That is called

Initiation, because that is where you will truly start to learn the things you need to learn in this life. The Voice indicates that you are ready.

'In the Tradition of the witches, an Initiation always takes place at the time of the Equinox, on the two days of the year when the days and the nights are equal in length. The next one is the Spring Equinox, on the twenty-first of March. I would like that to be the date of your Initiation because I, too, was initiated at the Spring Equinox. You know how to use the ritual instruments and you know all the rituals that keep open the bridge between the visible and the invisible. Whenever you perform one of those rituals, your soul recalls the lessons it learned in past lives.

'When you heard the Voice, you brought into the visible world something that was happening in the invisible world. In other words, you realised that your soul was ready for the next step. You have achieved your first major objective.'

It occurred to Brida that her original desire had been to see the point of light that would indicate her Soulmate, but she had been thinking a lot lately about the search for love, and that first desire was now dwindling in importance with each week that passed.

'There is just one test you must pass before you can be accepted for the Spring Initiation. If you fail, don't worry, you have many Equinoxes ahead of you, and one day you will be initiated. Up until now, you have dealt only with your masculine side: knowledge. You know certain things and are capable of understanding what you know, but you haven't yet touched on the one great feminine force, one of the great transformational powers. And knowledge without transformation is not wisdom.

'This force has always been an accursed Power among witches in general and women in particular. It is a force known to everyone on this planet. We women know that we are the great guardians of its secrets. Because of this force we are doomed to wander a dangerous, hostile world, because we were the ones who awoke it and because there have been places where it was considered an abomination. Anyone who comes into contact with this force, however unknowingly, is bound to it for the rest of their life. It can be your master or your slave; you can transform it into a magical force or use it all your life without ever realising its immense power. This force is in everything around us: it's in the visible world of ordinary people and in the invisible world of the mystics. It can be killed, crushed, hidden, even denied. It can lie dormant for years, forgotten in a corner somewhere; we can treat it in whichever way we want, but once someone has experienced this force, he or she will never be able to forget it.'

'What force is that?'

'Don't keep asking stupid questions,' retorted Wicca. 'You know perfectly well what that force is.'

Yes, Brida knew.

Sex.

Wicca drew aside one of the immaculately white curtains and showed Brida the view. The window looked out on the river, on old buildings, on distant hills. The Magus lived somewhere over there.

'What's that?' asked Wicca, pointing at the top of a church steeple.

'A cross. The symbol of Christianity.'

'A Roman would never enter a building with a cross on it. He would think it was a house of torture, because the cross represents one of the cruellest instruments of torture ever invented by man. The cross might not have changed, but its meaning certainly has. In the same way, when mankind was closer to God, sex was the symbolic means of communion with the divine, a re-encounter with the meaning of life.'

'Why do people seeking God so often distance themselves from sex?'

Wicca was irritated by the interruption, but she answered anyway.

'When I talk about the force, I'm not talking only about the sexual act. Some people make use of this force without actually having sex. Everything depends on which path you take.'

'I know that force,' Brida said. 'I know how to make use of it.'

'You may know about having sex with someone in bed, but that isn't the same as knowing it as a force. Both men and women are extremely vulnerable to the force of sex, because, during sex, pleasure and fear are present in equal measure.'

'Why do pleasure and fear go together?'

She had finally asked a question worth answering.

'Because anyone who comes into contact with sex knows that they're dealing with something which only happens in all its intensity when they lose control. When we're in bed with someone, we're giving permission to that person not only to commune with our body, but with our whole being. The pure forces of life are in communication with each other, independently of us, and then we cannot hide who we are.

'It doesn't matter what image we have of ourselves. It doesn't matter what disguises we put on, what smart answers or honourable excuses we give. During sex, it's very difficult to deceive the other person, because that is when each person shows who they really are.'

Wicca was speaking like someone who knew this force well. Her eyes were shining and there was pride in her voice. Perhaps that was what lay behind her continuing attractiveness. Brida was glad Wicca was her teacher, and one day she would discover the secret of that charm.

'Before the Initiation can take place, you have to experience that force. Everything else belongs to the Great Mysteries, and you will learn about that after the ceremony.'

'How do I go about experiencing it, then?'

'It's a simple enough formula, and like all simple things, its results are far more complex than all the complicated rituals I've taught you so far.'

Wicca came over to Brida, grasped her shoulders and looked into her eyes.

'This is the formula: use your five senses at all times. If they all come together at the moment of orgasm, you will be accepted for Initiation.'

I came to apologise,' Brida said.

They were in the same place where they had met before, near the rocks on the right-hand side of the mountain, from where you could see the valley below.

'Sometimes I think one thing and do another,' she went on. 'But if you've ever felt love, you'll know how painful it is to suffer for love.'

'Yes, I know,' replied the Magus. It was the first time he had made any comment on his private life.

'You were right about the point of light. It's not really that important. Now I've discovered that the search can be as interesting as actually finding what you're looking for.'

'As long as you can overcome your fear.'

'That's true.'

And Brida was pleased to know that even he, with all his knowledge, still felt fear.

* * *

They spent the afternoon walking through the snow-covered forest. They talked about plants, about the landscape, and about the ways in which the spiders in that region wove their webs. At one point, they met a shepherd leading his sheep back home.

'Hello, Santiago!' cried the Magus. Then he turned to her:

'God has a special fondness for shepherds. They are people accustomed to nature, silence, patience. They possess all the necessary virtues to commune with the Universe.'

Up until then, they hadn't discussed such matters at all, and Brida didn't want to anticipate the moment. She brought the conversation back to her life and to what was going on in the world. Her sixth sense told her to avoid mentioning Lorens. She didn't know what was going on, nor did she know why the Magus was being so attentive, but she needed to keep that flame alight. An accursed power, Wicca had called it. She had an objective and this was her one means of attaining it.

They passed a few sheep, whose feet left strange prints in the snow. This time there was no shepherd, but the sheep seemed to know where to go and what they were looking for. The Magus stood for a long time watching the sheep, as if he were studying some great secret from the Tradition of the Sun, one that Brida could not understand.

As the light began to fade, so did the feeling of terror and respect that always gripped her when she was with him. For the first time, she felt calm and confident by his side. Perhaps because she didn't need to demonstrate her gifts. She had heard the Voice, and her entry into the world of those other men and women was now simply a matter of time. She, too, belonged to the path of mysteries, and from the moment that she heard the Voice, the man beside her had become part of her Universe.

She felt like grasping his hands and asking him to show her some aspect of the Tradition of the Sun, just as she used to ask Lorens to talk to her about the ancient stars. It was a way of saying that they were seeing the same thing, albeit from different angles.

Something was telling her that he needed this, and it wasn't the mysterious Voice of the Tradition of the Moon, but the restless, sometimes foolish voice of her heart. A voice she didn't often listen to, since it always led her along paths she couldn't understand.

But emotions were, indeed, wild horses and they demanded to be heard. Brida let them run free for a while until they grew tired. Her emotions were telling her how good it would be that afternoon if she were in love with him, because when you were in love, you were capable of learning everything and of knowing things you had never dared even to think, because love was the key to the understanding of all the mysteries.

She ran through various amorous scenarios involving the Magus before she finally regained control. Then she said to herself that she could never love a man like him, because he understood the Universe, and all human feelings look small when viewed from a distance.

They reached the ruins of an old monastic church. The Magus sat down on one of the many piles of carved stone scattered on the ground, and Brida cleared the snow off a broad windowsill.

'It must be good to live here, spend all day in the forest and then go home to sleep in a nice warm house,' she said.

'Yes, it is good. I know the songs of all the different birds and I can read God's signs. I've learned the Traditions of the Sun and the Moon.'

'But I'm alone,' he felt like adding. 'And there's no point in understanding the entire Universe if you're alone.'

There, perched on the windowsill, was his Other Half. He could see the point of light above her left shoulder, and he regretted ever having learned the two Traditions, because had it not been for the point of light he might not have fallen in love with her.

'She's intelligent. She sensed the danger early, and now wants to know nothing more about points of light,' he thought.

'I heard the Voice. Wicca really is an excellent teacher.'

It was the first time that afternoon that she'd brought up the subject of magic.

'The Voice will teach you the mysteries of the world, the mysteries that are imprisoned in time, and which are carried from generation to generation by witches.'

He spoke without really listening to what he was saying. He was trying to remember when he had first met his Soulmate. Solitary people lose track of time, the hours are long and the days interminable. Even so, he knew they had only been together twice before. Brida was learning very fast.

'I know the rituals and I'm to be initiated into the Great Mysteries at the Spring Equinox.'

She was beginning to feel tense again.

'There's one thing, though, that I still haven't experienced – the force that everyone knows and which they revere as if it were a mystery.'

The Magus understood why she had come that afternoon. It wasn't just to walk among the trees and leave two sets of footprints in the snow, footprints that were getting closer every minute.

Brida turned up her jacket collar to protect her face, whether because the cold grew more intense when they stopped walking or whether she was merely trying to conceal her nervousness, she wasn't sure.

'I want to learn how to awaken the force of sex through the five senses,' she said at last. 'Wicca won't talk about it. She says that I'll discover it just as I discovered the Voice.'

They sat for a few minutes in silence. She wondered if she should even be talking about such a thing in the ruins of a church. But then she remembered that there are many ways of using the force. The monks who had lived there had worked through abstinence, and they would understand what she meant.

'I've tried all kinds of things. I think there must be a trick, like the trick with the phone to get me to really see the tarot cards. I think it's something Wicca doesn't want to teach me. I think she must have found it very hard to learn and wants me to experience the same difficulties.'

'Was that why you came looking for me?'

Brida looked deep into his eyes.

'Yes.'

*　*　*

She hoped her answer would convince him, but she wasn't sure of anything any more. The walk through the snowy wood, the sunlight on the snow, the easy conversation about the ordinary things of the world, all of this had set her emotions galloping like wild horses. She had to persuade herself again that she was there for only one reason, and that she would attain her objective by whatever means possible. Because God had been a woman before he became a man.

The Magus got up from the pile of stones he was sitting on and walked over to the only wall that had not crumbled into rubble. In the middle of the wall was a door, and he stood leaning against it. The evening sun lit him from behind and Brida could not see his face.

'There's one thing that Wicca didn't teach you,' he said. 'She may have forgotten to do so, or she may have wanted you to discover it alone.'

'Well, here I am, alone.'

And she asked herself if perhaps this had been her teacher's plan all along, to bring her together with this man.

'I'm going to teach you,' he said at last. 'Come with me.'

They walked to a place where the trees were taller and their trunks thicker. Brida noticed that some of them had rough-and-ready ladders attached to the trunks. At the top of each ladder was a kind of cabin.

'This must be where the hermits of the Tradition of the Sun live,' she thought.

The Magus carefully examined each cabin, chose one and asked Brida to join him.

She started to climb. Halfway up, she felt afraid, because a fall might prove fatal. Nevertheless, she resolved to go on; she was in a sacred place, protected by the spirits of the forest. The Magus had not asked if she wanted to do this, but perhaps this was considered unnecessary in the Tradition of the Sun.

When they reached the top, she gave a long sigh. She had conquered another of her fears.

'This is a good place to teach you the path,' he said. 'A place of ambush.'

'Ambush?'

'These cabins are used by hunters. They have to be high up so that the animals don't catch the hunters' scent. During the year, the hunters leave food on the ground so that the animals get used to coming here, and then one day, they kill them.'

Brida noticed some empty cartridges on the floor. She was shocked.

'Look down,' he said.

There was barely enough space for two people, and his body was almost touching hers. She did as he asked. The tree must have been one of the tallest, because she could see the tops of the other trees, the valley, the snow-covered mountains on the horizon. It was beautiful there; he needn't have said what he did about it being a place of ambush.

The Magus pushed back the canvas roof, and suddenly the cabin was filled with sunlight. It was cold, and it seemed to Brida that they were in a magical place, on the top of the world. Her emotions wanted to set off again at a gallop, but she had to keep them in check.

'I didn't need to bring you here in order to explain what you want to know,' said the Magus, 'but I wanted you to understand a little more about this forest. In the winter, when both hunter and hunted are far away, I come and climb these trees and contemplate the Earth.'

He really did want to share his world with her. Brida's blood began to flow more quickly. She felt at peace, immersed in one of those moments in life when the only possible alternative is to lose all control.

* * *

'Our relationships with the world come through our five senses. Plunging into the world of magic means discovering other unknown senses, and sex propels us towards one of those doors.'

He was speaking more loudly now. He sounded like a teacher giving a biology lesson. 'Perhaps it's better like this,' she thought, although she was not convinced.

'It doesn't matter whether you're seeking wisdom or pleasure through the force of sex, it will always be a total experience, because it's the only experience that touches – or should touch – all five senses at once. All our channels with the other person are wide open.

'At the moment of orgasm, the five senses vanish, and you enter the world of magic; you can no longer see, hear, taste, touch or smell. During those long seconds everything disappears, to be replaced by ecstasy. It is exactly the same ecstasy as that attained by mystics after years of renunciation and discipline.'

Brida felt like asking why the mystics hadn't tried to attain it through orgasm, then she remembered that some were the descendants of angels.

'What propels a person towards this ecstasy are the five senses. The more the senses are stimulated, the stronger will be the drive towards ecstasy and the more powerful the ecstasy. Do you understand?'

Of course she understood. She nodded. But that question left her feeling more distant. She wished he were still strolling by her side through the forest.

'That's all there is to it.'

'I know all that, but I still can't do it.' Brida didn't dare mention Lorens. She sensed it would be dangerous. 'You told me that there's a way to achieve it.'

She was nervous and upset. Her emotions were beginning to gallop out of control.

The Magus looked down again at the forest below. Brida wondered if he, too, was struggling with his emotions, but she didn't want to believe in what she was thinking, nor should she.

She knew what the Tradition of the Sun was. She knew that its Teachers taught through space and time. She had thought about this before she first searched him out. She had imagined that they might one day be together as they were now, with no one else near. That is how the Teachers of the Tradition of the Sun were – always teaching through action and never giving theory undue importance. She had thought all this before ever coming to the forest, but she had come anyway, because now her path was more important than anything else. She needed to continue the tradition of her many lives.

But now he was behaving like Wicca, who only talked about things.

'Teach me,' she said.

The Magus was staring at the bare, snowy branches. He could, at that moment, forget he was a Teacher and be merely a Magus, a man like any other man. He knew that his Soulmate was there before him. He could talk about the point of light he could see, and she would believe him, and their re-encounter would be complete. Even if she left in tears, she would come back eventually, because he was telling the truth – and she needed him as much as he needed her. That was the wisdom of Soulmates: they always recognised each other.

But he was a Teacher, and one day, in a village in Spain, he had sworn a sacred oath. That oath said, amongst other things, that no Teacher should ever force another person to make a choice. He had made that mistake once and because of that had spent all those years in exile from the world. Now it was different, but he still didn't want to take the risk. For a moment, he thought: 'I could give up magic for her,' but immediately realised how foolish that thought was. Love didn't require that kind of renunciation. True love allowed each person to follow their own path, knowing that they would never lose touch with their Soulmate.

He must be patient. He must remember the patience of shepherds and know that, sooner or later, they would be together. That was the Law. And he had believed in that Law all his life.

'What you're asking me is very simple,' he said at last. He had mastered his emotions; discipline had won out.

'Make sure that when you touch the other person, all your five senses are working, because sex has a life of its own. The moment you begin, you're no longer in control; it takes control of you. And whatever you bring to it – your fears, your desires, your sensibility – will remain. That's why people become impotent. When you have sex, take with you to bed only love and your senses, all five of them. Only then will you experience communion with God.'

Brida looked down at the cartridges on the floor. She did not betray her feelings for an instant. She knew what the trick was now, and that, she said to herself, was all she was interested in.

'That's all I can teach you.'

She did not move. The wild horses were being tamed by the silence.

'Take seven deep, calm breaths and make sure all your senses are working before there's any physical contact. Just let things take their course.'

He was a Teacher of the Tradition of the Sun. He had come through yet another test. His Soulmate was also teaching him things.

'Right, I've shown you the view from up here. We can go down now.'

She sat distractedly watching the children playing in the square. Someone had told her once that every city has a 'magic place', a place where we go when we need to think seriously about life. That square was her 'magic place' in Dublin. It was near the apartment she'd rented when she first arrived, full of dreams and expectations. Her plan then had been to enrol as a student at Trinity College and eventually become a professor of literature. She used to spend a lot of time on that bench, writing poetry and generally trying to behave as her literary idols had.

But the money her father sent wasn't enough and she'd had to take a job at the import–export company where she worked now. Not that she minded; she was happy with what she was doing, and in fact her job was one of the most important things in her life, because it gave a sense of reality to everything and kept her from going mad. It allowed her to maintain a precarious balance between the visible world and the invisible.

The children continued to play. Like her, all of them had

once been told stories about fairies and witches, about witches who dressed all in black and offered poisoned apples to poor young girls lost in the forest. None of those children could possibly imagine that a real, live witch was watching them playing now.

That afternoon, Wicca had asked her to try an exercise entirely unrelated to the Tradition of the Moon, an exercise useful to anyone wishing to keep open the bridge between the visible and the invisible.

It was simple enough. She had to lie down, relax and imagine one of the main shopping areas in the city. Then she had to concentrate on one particular shop window and notice every detail of what was in the window, where it was, and how much each thing cost. When she had finished the exercise, she had to go to the street and see if she had been right.

Now she was there in the square watching the children. She had just come back from the shop, and the shop window had been exactly as she'd imagined it. She wondered if this really was an exercise for ordinary people, or if her months of training as a witch had helped. She would never know.

But the shopping street she had imagined was very near to her 'magic place'. 'Nothing happens by chance,' she thought. Her heart was troubled over a matter she could not resolve: Love. She loved Lorens, she was sure of that. She knew that when she was an adept in the Tradition of the Moon, she would see the point of light above his left shoulder. One afternoon, when they'd gone to a café together to drink a cup of hot chocolate near the tower that had inspired James Joyce's *Ulysses*, she had seen that special light in his eyes.

The Magus was right. The Tradition of the Sun was the path of all men, and it was there so that it could be deciphered by anyone who knew how to pray and be patient and who wanted to learn what it had to teach. The more she immersed herself in the Tradition of the Moon, the more she understood and admired the Tradition of the Sun.

The Magus. She was thinking about him again. This was the problem that had brought her back to her 'magic place'. She had thought about him often since that visit to the hunters' cabin. She would like to be there right now so that she could tell him about this latest exercise, but she knew that was just a pretext; what she really wanted was for him to invite her to go for a walk in the forest again. She was sure he would be pleased to see her, and she was beginning to believe, for some mysterious reason – which she didn't even dare to think about – that he enjoyed her company too.

'I've always had too vivid an imagination,' she thought, trying to get the Magus out of her head, but knowing that he would soon be back.

She didn't want to keep thinking about him. She was a woman and familiar with the symptoms of falling in love, something which she had to avoid at all costs. She loved Lorens and wanted things to continue as they were. Her world had changed quite enough.

On Saturday morning, Lorens phoned.

'Let's go for a walk along the cliffs,' he said.

Brida prepared something to eat, and together they endured the long journey in an inadequately heated bus. They reached the village at around midday.

Brida felt excited. In her first year as a student of literature at the university, she had read a lot about the poet who had lived there. He was a mysterious man, who knew a great deal about the Tradition of the Moon; he had been a member of secret societies and left in his books a hidden message for those who seek the spiritual path. His name was W.B. Yeats. She remembered two particular lines by him, which seemed just made for that cold morning, with the seagulls flying over the boats anchored in the little harbour:

I have spread my dreams under your feet;
Tread softly because you tread on my dreams.

They went into the only pub in the village, drank a whiskey to keep out the cold, and then set off. The little tarmac road gave way to a steep climb, and half an hour later they reached what the locals called 'the cliffs'. This was a promontory made up of rocky outcrops that dropped sheer into the sea. There was a path to follow and, even at a leisurely pace, they would be able do the whole walk in less than four hours and still catch the bus back to Dublin.

Brida was delighted at the prospect. Regardless of what emotions life might be holding in reserve for her that year, she always found the winter hard to bear. All she did was go to work during the day, to the university in the evening and to the cinema at weekends. She dutifully performed the rituals and dances Wicca had taught her, but she had a yearning to be out in the world, to see a little nature.

It was overcast and the clouds were very low, but the physical exercise and the whiskey helped fend off the cold. The path was too narrow for them to walk along side by side; Lorens went ahead, and Brida followed a little way behind. It was hard to talk in these circumstances. Nevertheless, they managed to exchange a few words, enough for them to feel each other close and to enjoy the nature around them.

She was gazing with childlike fascination at the landscape. It must have been exactly the same thousands of years ago, in an age when there were no towns, no harbours, no poets, no young women seeking the Tradition of the Moon; then there were only the rocks, the crashing waves, and the seagulls drifting about beneath the low clouds. Now and then, Brida peered over the precipice and felt slightly dizzy. The sea was saying things she couldn't understand; the seagulls were making patterns she couldn't follow. And yet she was looking at that primitive world as if the true wisdom of the Universe lay there rather than in any of the books she'd read or in any of the rituals she practised. As they moved away from the harbour, everything else gradually diminished in importance – her dreams, her daily life, her search. There was only what Wicca called 'God's signature'.

All that remained was that primitive moment among the pure forces of nature, the sense of being alive and in the company of someone she loved.

After nearly two hours of walking, the path suddenly grew wider, and they decided to sit down together to rest. They couldn't stop for long. The cold would soon become unbearable and they would have to move on, but she felt like spending at least a few minutes by his side, looking up at the clouds and listening to the sound of the sea.

Brida could smell the sea air and was aware of the taste of salt in her mouth. She warmed her face against Lorens' jacket. It was a moment of great plenitude. All five of her senses were working.

Yes, all five of her senses were working.

For a fraction of a second, the thought of the Magus entered her mind and then vanished. All she cared about now were those five senses. They must keep working. This was the moment.

'I need to talk to you, Lorens.'

Lorens murmured something or other, but his heart was afraid. As he looked up at the clouds or down at the precipice, he realised that this woman was the most important thing in his life; that she was the explanation, the sole reason for the existence of those rocks, that sky, that winter. If she were not there with him, it wouldn't matter if all the angels of heaven came flying down to comfort him – Paradise would make no sense.

'I want to tell you that I love you,' Brida said softly. 'Because you've shown me the joy of love.'

She felt full, complete, as if the whole landscape were seeping into her soul. He began stroking her hair. And she was sure that, if she took a risk, she would experience love as never before.

Brida kissed him. She felt the taste of his mouth, the touch of his tongue. She was aware of every movement and sensed that he was feeling exactly the same, because the Tradition of the Sun always reveals itself to those who look at the world as if they were seeing it for the first time.

'I want to make love with you right here, Lorens.'

Various thoughts flashed through his mind: they were on a public footpath, someone might come by, some other person crazy enough to visit this place in the middle of winter. But anyone crazy enough to do so would also be able to understand that certain forces, once set in motion, cannot be interrupted.

He slipped his hands under her sweater and stroked her breasts. Brida surrendered herself entirely. The forces of the world were penetrating her five senses and these were becoming transformed into an overwhelming energy. They lay down on the ground between the rock, the precipice and the sea, between the life of the seagulls flying up above and the death of the stones beneath. And they began, fearlessly, to make love, because God protects the innocent.

They no longer felt the cold. Their blood was flowing so fast in their veins that she tore off some of her clothes and so did he. There was no more pain; knees and back were pressed into the stony ground, but that became part of their pleasure, completing it. Brida knew that she was close to orgasm, but it was still a very remote feeling, because she was entirely connected to the world: her body and Lorens' body mingled with the sea and the stones, with life and death. She remained in that state for as long as possible, while some part of her was vaguely conscious that she was doing things she had never done before. What she was feeling, though, was the bringing together once more of herself and the meaning of life; it was a return to the garden of Eden; it was the moment when Eve was reabsorbed into Adam's body and the two halves became Creation.

At last, she could no longer control the world around her, her five senses seemed to break free and she wasn't strong enough to hold on to them. As if struck by a sacred bolt of lightning, she unleashed them, and the world, the seagulls, the taste of salt, the hard earth, the smell of the sea, the clouds, all disappeared, and in their place appeared a vast golden light, which grew and grew until it touched the most distant star in the galaxy.

She gradually came down from that state, and the sea and the clouds reappeared, but everything was filled by a sense of profound peace, the peace of a universe which became, if only for a matter of moments, explicable, because she was in communion with the world. She had discovered another bridge that joined the visible to the invisible, and she would never again forget the path that led to it.

The following day, she phoned Wicca and told her what had happened. For a while, Wicca said nothing.

'Congratulations,' she said at last. 'You've made it.'

She explained that, from then on, the power of sex would bring about profound changes in the way Brida saw and experienced the world.

'You're ready now for the celebration of the Equinox. There's just one more thing.'

'One more thing? But you said that was it!'

'It's quite easy. You simply have to dream of a dress, the dress you will wear on the day.'

'And what if I can't.'

'You will. You've done the most difficult part.'

And then, as so often, she changed the subject. She told Brida that she'd bought a new car and needed to do some shopping. Would Brida like to go with her?

Brida was proud to be invited and asked her boss if she could leave work early. It was the first time Wicca had shown her any kind of affection, even if it was only an invitation to join her on a shopping trip. She knew that many of Wicca's other students would love to be in her shoes.

Perhaps that afternoon would provide her with a chance to show Wicca how important she was to her and how much she wanted to be her friend. It was difficult for Brida to separate friendship from the spiritual search, and she was hurt because, up until then, her teacher had never shown the slightest interest in her private life. Their conversations never went beyond what Brida needed to know in order to work within the Tradition of the Moon.

At the appointed hour, Wicca was waiting outside in a red MG convertible, with the top down. The car, a British classic, was exceptionally well preserved, with gleaming bodywork and a polished wooden dashboard. Brida didn't even dare hazard a guess at how much it must have cost. The idea that a witch should own such an expensive car frightened her a little. Before she'd known anything about the Tradition of the Moon, she'd heard all kinds of tales in her childhood about witches making terrible pacts with the Devil in exchange for money and power.

'Isn't it a bit cold to drive with the top down?' she asked as she got in.

'I can't wait until summer,' Wicca said, 'I just can't. I've been aching to go for a drive like this for ages.'

That was good. At least, in this respect, she was like any other normal person.

They drove through the streets, receiving admiring glances from older passers-by and a few wolf-whistles and compliments from men.

'It's a good sign that you're worried about not being able to dream about the dress,' said Wicca. Brida, however, had already forgotten about their phone conversation.

'Never stop having doubts. If you ever do, it will be because you've stopped moving forward, and at that point, God will step in and pull the rug from under your feet, because that is His way of controlling His chosen ones, by making sure they always follow their appointed path to the end. If, for any reason, we stop, whether out of complacency, laziness, or out of a mistaken belief that we know enough, He forces us on.

'On the other hand, you must be careful never to allow doubt to paralyse you. Always take the decisions you need to take, even if you're not sure you're doing the right thing. You'll never go wrong if, when you make a decision, you keep in mind an old German proverb that the Tradition of the Moon has adopted: "The Devil is in the detail". Remember that proverb and you'll always be able to turn a wrong decision into a right one.'

Wicca suddenly stopped outside a garage.

'There's a superstition connected to that proverb too,' she said. 'It only comes to our aid when we need it. I've just bought this car, and the devil is in the detail.'

She got out as soon as a mechanic came over to her.

'Is the hood broken, Madam?'

Wicca didn't even answer. She asked him to check the car over for her, and while he was working, the two women sat and drank hot chocolate in a café over the way.

'Watch what the mechanic does,' Wicca said, looking across

at the garage. He had the bonnet open and was standing staring at the engine, not even moving.

'He's not touching anything. He's just looking. He's done this job for years, and he knows that the car speaks to him in a special language. It's not his reason that's working now, it's his intuition.'

Suddenly, the mechanic went straight to one particular part of the engine and starting fiddling with it.

'He's found the fault,' Wicca went on. 'He didn't waste a moment, because between him and the car there is perfect communication. Every good mechanic I've ever known has been the same.'

'So have the mechanics I've known,' thought Brida, but she'd always assumed they behaved that way because they didn't know where to start. She'd never noticed that they always started in the right place.

'If they have the wisdom of the Sun in their lives, why don't they try to understand the fundamental questions of the Universe? Why do they prefer to fix cars or work in a bar serving coffee?'

'And what makes you think that we, with our path and our dedication, understand the Universe any better than other people?

'I have many students. They're all perfectly ordinary people, who cry at the movies and worry if their children are late home, even though they know that death is not the end. Witchcraft is merely one way of being close to the Supreme Wisdom, but anything you do can lead you there, as long as you work with love in your heart. We witches can converse with the Soul of the World, see the point of light above the left shoulder of our Soulmate, and contemplate the infinite through the glow and silence of a candle, but we don't understand car engines. Mechanics need us as much as we need them. They find their bridge across to the invisible in a car engine, while we find ours in the Tradition of the Moon, but the bridge connects to the same invisible world.

'Play your part and don't worry about what others do. Believe that God also speaks to them, and that they are as engaged as you are in discovering the meaning of life.'

'The car's fine,' said the mechanic, when they went back to the garage, 'apart from a hose that was about to burst. And that could have caused you serious problems.'

Wicca haggled a little over the price, but she was very glad that she'd remembered the proverb.

They went to one of Dublin's main shopping streets, which also happened to be the location of the shop that Brida had once had to visualise as part of an exercise. Whenever the conversation turned to personal topics, Wicca would respond vaguely or evasively, but she spoke with great verve about trivial matters – prices, clothes, rude shop assistants. Everything she bought that afternoon revealed sophistication and good taste.

Brida knew that it wasn't the done thing to ask someone where she got her money, but so great was her curiosity that she came very close to violating that most elementary rule of politeness.

They ended up in a Japanese restaurant, with a dish of sashimi before them.

'May God bless our food,' said Wicca. 'We are all sailors on an unknown sea; may He make us brave enough to accept this mystery.'

'But you're a Teacher of the Tradition of the Moon,' said Brida. 'You know the answers.'

Wicca sat for a moment, absorbed, looking at the food. Then she said:

'I know how to travel between the present and the past. I know the world of the spirits, and I've communed with forces so amazing that no words in any language could describe them. I could perhaps say that I possess the silent knowledge of the journey that has brought the human race to where it is at this moment.

'But because I know all this, and because I am a Teacher, I also know that we will never ever know the ultimate reason for our existence. We might know the how, where and when of being here, but the why will always be a question that remains unanswered. The main objective of the great Architect of the Universe is known to Him alone, and to no one else.'

A silence fell.

'Right now, while we're here eating, ninety-nine per cent of the people on this planet are, in their own way, struggling with that very question. Why are we here? Many think they've found the answer in religion or in materialism. Others despair and spend their lives and their money trying to grasp the meaning of it all. A few let the question go unanswered and live for the moment, regardless of the results or the consequences.

'Only the brave and those who understand the Traditions of the Sun and the Moon are aware that the only possible answer to the question is I DON'T KNOW.

'This might, at first, seem frightening, leaving us terribly vulnerable in our dealings with the world, with the things of the world and with our own sense of our existence. Once we've got over that initial fear, however, we gradually become accustomed to the only possible solution: to follow our dreams. Having the courage to take the steps we always wanted to take is the only way of showing that we trust in God.

'As soon as we accept this, life takes on a sacred meaning, and we experience the same emotion the Virgin must have felt when, one afternoon in her otherwise very ordinary existence, a stranger appeared to her and made her an offer. "Be it unto me according to thy word," said the Virgin. Because she had understood that the greatest thing a human being can do is to accept the Mystery.'

After another long silence, Wicca again took up her knife and fork and resumed her meal. Brida looked at her, proud to be by her side. She wasn't bothered now by the questions she would never ask, about how Wicca earned her money or if she was in love with someone or jealous of someone else. She thought about the greatness of soul of the true sages, sages who had spent their entire life searching for an answer that did not exist, but who were not tempted to invent an answer when they realised there was none. Instead, they carried on humbly inhabiting a Universe they would never understand. The only way they could truly participate was by following their own desires, their own dreams, because that is how man becomes an instrument of God.

'So what's the point of looking for an answer then?'

'We don't look for an answer, we accept, and then life becomes much more intense, much more brilliant, because we understand that each minute, each step that we take, has a meaning that goes far beyond us as individuals. We realise that somewhere in time and space this question *does* have an answer. We realise that there is a reason for us being here, and for us, that is enough.

'We plunge into the Dark Night with faith, we fulfil what the ancient alchemists used to call our Personal Legend and we surrender ourselves fully to each moment, knowing that there is always a hand to guide us, and whether we accept it or not is entirely up to us.'

That night, Brida spent hours listening to music, entirely given over to the miracle of being alive. She thought about her favourite authors. One of them – the English poet William Blake – had, with just one simple phrase, given her enough faith to go in search of wisdom.

What is now proved was once only imagin'd.

It was time to perform one of her rituals. She would spend the next few minutes contemplating a candle flame, and to do so, she sat down before the little altar. The process of contemplation took her back to the afternoon when she and Lorens had made love among the rocks. There were seagulls flying as high as the clouds and as low as the waves.

The fish must have asked themselves how they managed to fly, these mysterious creatures who plunged into their world, then left as quickly as they entered.

The birds must have asked themselves how the creatures they fed on and that lived beneath the waves could possibly manage to breathe under water.

Birds existed and fish existed. Theirs were universes that occasionally collided, but they could not answer each other's questions. And yet both had questions, and the questions had answers.

Brida looked at the flame before her, and a magical atmosphere began to grow around her. This was what normally happened, but that night, the feeling was more intense.

If she were capable of asking a question, it was because, in another Universe, there was an answer. Someone knew it, even if she didn't. She didn't need to understand the meaning of life; it was enough to find someone who did, and then fall asleep in his arms and sleep as a child sleeps, knowing that someone stronger than you is protecting you from all evil and all danger.

When the ritual was over, she said a little prayer in gratitude for the steps she had so far taken. She was grateful because the first person she had asked about magic hadn't tried to explain the Universe to her; instead, he had made her spend the whole night in a dark forest.

She needed to go there and thank him for all he had taught her.

Whenever she went in search of that man, she was looking for something; whenever she found that something, all she did was leave, often without even saying goodbye. But he had shown her the door through which she hoped to pass at the next Equinox. She should at least say 'Thank you'.

No, she wasn't afraid of falling in love with him. She had read things in Lorens' eyes about the hidden side of her own soul, and while she might have her doubts about being able to dream of a dress, as regards his love, about that she was perfectly clear.

Thank you for accepting my invitation,' she said to the Magus when they sat down. They were sitting in the only pub in the village, which is where she had first noticed the strange light in his eyes.

The Magus said nothing. He noticed that her energy was quite different now; she had clearly managed to awaken the Force.

'On the night you left me alone in the forest, I promised that I'd come back either to thank you or to curse you. I promised that I'd come back when I found my path. But I didn't keep either of those promises. I always came in search of help, and you never let me down. It may be presumptuous of me, but I want you to know that you have acted as God's instrument, and I would like you to be my guest tonight.'

Just as she was about to order two whiskies, he got up, went over to the bar and returned carrying two bottles, one of wine and one of mineral water, and two glasses.

'In Ancient Persia,' he said, 'when two people met to drink

together, one of them was chosen to be King of the Night, usually the person who was paying.'

He didn't know if his voice sounded sufficiently steady. He was a man in love, and Brida's energy had changed.

He placed the wine and the mineral water before her.

'It was up to the King of the Night to set the tone of the conversation. If he poured more water than wine into the first glass to be drunk, that meant he wished to speak of serious things. If he poured equal quantities of both, they would speak of both serious and pleasant things. Finally, if he filled the glass with wine and added only a few drops of water, the night would be relaxing and enjoyable.'

Brida filled the glasses to the brim with wine and added only a drop of water to each.

'I came to say thank you,' she said again, 'for teaching me that life is an act of faith, and that I am worthy of the search. That has helped me enormously on the path I've chosen.'

They both drained that first glass quickly. He because he was feeling tense. She because she was feeling relaxed.

'Only light subjects, all right?' Brida said.

The Magus said that since she was the King of the Night, it was up to her to decide what they should talk about.

'I want to know a little about your personal life. I want to know if you ever had an affair with Wicca.'

He nodded. Brida felt an inexplicable tremor of jealousy, but she wasn't sure whether she felt jealous of him or of Wicca.

'But we never considered living together,' he said. They both knew the two Traditions. They both knew that they were not each other's Soulmate.

'I didn't want to learn how to see the point of light,' thought Brida, but she saw now that this was inevitable. That was what love between witches was like.

She drank a little more. She was getting closer to her objective; it would not be long now until the Spring Equinox, and she could afford to relax. It had been a long time since she had allowed herself to drink more than she should, but now, all she had to do was dream of a dress.

They continued talking and drinking. Brida wanted to return to the subject of Wicca, but she needed him to be more relaxed too. She kept both their glasses filled, and they finished the first bottle while in the middle of a conversation about the difficulties of living in such a small village. The locals associated the Magus with the devil.

Brida was pleased to feel important to him; he must be very lonely. Maybe no one in the village ever addressed more than a few polite words to him. They opened another bottle, and she was surprised to see that a Magus, a man who spent all day in the forest seeking communion with God was also capable of drinking and getting drunk.

By the time they had finished the second bottle, she had forgotten that she was there in order to thank the man sitting opposite her. Her relationship with him – she realised now – had always been a veiled challenge. She didn't want to see him as an ordinary person, but she was getting dangerously close to doing just that. She preferred the image of the wise man who had led her to a cabin high up in the trees and who often spent hours contemplating the sunset.

She began to talk about Wicca, to see how he reacted. She said what an excellent Teacher she was and how she had taught her everything she needed to know so far, but in such a subtle way that it was if she'd always known the things she was learning.

'But you have,' said the Magus. 'That is the Tradition of the Sun.'

'He's obviously not going to admit that Wicca is a good teacher,' thought Brida. She drank another glass of wine and continued to talk about her Teacher, but the Magus made no further comment.

'Tell me about you and her,' she said, to see if she could provoke him. She didn't want to know, she really didn't, but it was the best way to get a reaction.

'A case of young love. We were part of a generation that knew no limits, the generation of the Beatles and the Rolling Stones.'

She was surprised to hear this. Far from relaxing her, the wine was making her tense. She still wanted to ask those questions, but now she realised that she wasn't happy with the answers.

'That was when we met,' he went on, unaware of her feelings. 'We were both seeking our respective paths, and they crossed when we happened to go to the same Teacher. Together we learned about the Tradition of the Sun and the Tradition of the Moon, and both, in our own fashion, became Teachers.'

Brida decided to pursue the subject. Two bottles of wine can make complete strangers feel as if they have been friends from childhood; wine gives people courage.

'Why did you split up?'

It was the Magus's turn to order another bottle. She noticed this and grew even more tense. She would hate to find out that he was still in love with Wicca.

'We split up when we learned about Soulmates.'

'If you hadn't found out about those points of light or the special light in your Soulmate's eyes, would you still be together?'

'I don't know. I only know that if we were, it wouldn't work for either of us. We only understand life and the Universe when we find our Soulmate.'

Brida paused for a moment, suddenly lost for words. It was the Magus who took up the conversation.

'Let's go,' he said, after taking only a sip of the wine from that third bottle. 'I need to feel the wind and the cold air on my face.'

'He's getting drunk,' she thought. 'And he's afraid.' She felt proud of herself; she could take her drink better than he could, and she wasn't in the least afraid of losing control. She had come out that night intending to enjoy herself.

'Just a little more. After all, I'm the King of the Night.'

The Magus drank another glass, but he knew he had reached his limit.

'You haven't asked me anything about myself,' she said challengingly. 'Aren't you curious? Or can you use your powers to see right through me?'

For a fraction of a second, she felt she had gone too far, but then she dismissed the thought. She merely noticed a change in the Magus's eyes; there was a completely different light in them now. Something in Brida seemed to open, or, rather, she had the sense of a wall coming down, a feeling that, from then on, everything would be permitted. She remembered the last time they had been together, her desire to stay with him, and his coldness. Now she understood that she hadn't gone there that night in order to thank him, but to seek revenge: to tell him that she'd discovered the Force with another man, a man she loved.

'Why do I need revenge? Why am I angry with him?' she wondered, but the wine wouldn't allow her to answer those questions coherently.

The Magus was looking at the young woman opposite him, and the desire to demonstrate his Power kept coming and going in his mind. On a night very like this, many years ago, his whole life had changed. It might have been the age of the Beatles and the Rolling Stones, but there were also people around at the time in search of unknown forces, forces they didn't even believe in. They made use of magical powers, all the while thinking that they were stronger than the powers themselves, convinced that they'd be able to leave the Tradition as soon as boredom set in. He had been one of those people. He had entered the sacred world through the Tradition of the Moon, learning rituals and crossing the bridge that connects the visible and the invisible.

At first, he dabbled in these powers on his own, learning from books, with no help from anyone. Then he met his Teacher. At their first meeting, his Teacher told him that he would be better off learning through the Tradition of the Sun, but the Magus didn't want that. The Tradition of the Moon was more interesting; it involved performing ancient rituals and learning the wisdom of time. And so his Teacher taught him the Tradition of the Moon, saying that perhaps this was the path that would eventually lead him to the Tradition of the Sun.

At the time, he was utterly sure of himself, of life, and of his conquests. A brilliant career lay ahead of him, and he intended using the Tradition of the Moon to achieve his goals. In order to do so, witchcraft demanded that he first become a Teacher, and that he never infringe the one limitation placed on all Teachers of the Tradition of the Moon: never to interfere with another person's free will. He could forge his own path in the world by using his magical knowledge, but he couldn't get rid of someone simply because they were in his way nor could he force them to follow him on his path. That was the one prohibition, the only tree of whose fruit he must not eat.

And everything went smoothly until he fell in love with one of his Teacher's other students, and she fell in love with him. Both knew the Traditions; he knew that he was not her man, and she knew that she was not his woman. Nevertheless, they surrendered to their love, leaving life in charge of separating them when the time came. Far from diminishing their passion, this only made them live each moment as if it were their last, and the love between them had all the intensity of things that take on an eternal quality precisely because they're going to die.

Then one day, she met another man. This man knew nothing of the Traditions, nor did he have a point of light above his left shoulder or the special light in his eyes that reveals someone to be your Soulmate. Love, however, is no respecter of reasons, and she fell in love; as far as she was concerned, her time with the Magus had come to an end.

They quarrelled and fought; he begged and implored. He subjected himself to all the usual humiliations endured by people in love. He learned things he never dreamed he would learn: hope, fear, acceptance. 'He doesn't have the point of light above his left shoulder,' he argued, 'you told me that yourself.' But she didn't care. Before she did finally meet her Soulmate, she wanted to know other men, to experience the world.

The Magus set a limit on his pain. When he reached it, he would forget all about her. For a reason he could now no longer remember, he did reach that limit, but instead of forgetting her, he discovered that his Teacher was right – emotions were like wild horses and it required wisdom to be able to control them. His passion was stronger than all his years of studying the Tradition of the Moon, stronger than all the mind-control techniques he had learned, stronger than the rigid discipline to which he'd had to submit in order to get where he was. Passion was a blind force, and it kept whispering in his ear that he must not lose that woman.

He could do nothing against her; she was a Teacher, like him, and she had learned her trade over many incarnations, some filled with fame and glory, others marked by fire and suffering. She would know how to defend herself.

However, there was a third party involved in this furious struggle. A man caught in destiny's mysterious web, a web that neither Magi nor Witches can understand. An ordinary man, perhaps as in love with that woman as he was, a man who wanted her to be happy and to do his best for her. An ordinary man, whom Providence's mysterious designs had thrown into the middle of this battle between a man and a woman who knew the Tradition of the Moon.

One night, when he could stand the pain no longer, he ate of the forbidden fruit. Using the power and knowledge that the wisdom of Time had taught him, he removed that man from the woman he loved.

He did not know to this day whether or not she ever found out, but it may well be that she had already grown tired of her new conquest and didn't much mind him leaving. However, his Teacher knew. His Teacher always knew everything, and the Tradition of the Moon was implacable with those Initiates who used Black Magic, especially to influence that most important and most vulnerable of human emotions: Love.

When he confronted his Teacher, he understood that the sacred vow he had made was impossible to break. He understood that the forces he thought he could control and use were far more powerful than he was. He understood that he was on his chosen path, but that it was not a path like any other. And he understood that in this incarnation he could never leave that path.

Now that he had erred, he had to pay a price, and the price was to drink that cruellest of poisons – loneliness – until Love felt that he had once more been transformed into a Teacher. Then, the same Love that he had wounded would set him free again and finally reveal his Soulmate to him.

You haven't asked me anything about myself. Aren't you curious? Or can you use your powers to see right through me?'

His past took no more than a second to flash through his mind, just long enough for him to decide whether to allow things to happen as they would in the Tradition of the Sun or to speak to her about the point of light and thus interfere in fate.

Brida wanted to be a witch, but she hadn't yet achieved that ambition. He remembered the cabin high up in the tree, when he had come very close to telling her; now he was tempted again, because, having lowered his guard, he had forgotten that the Devil is in the detail. We are all masters of our own destiny. We can so easily make the same mistakes over and over. We can so easily flee from everything that we desire and which life so generously places before us.

Alternatively, we can surrender ourselves to Divine Providence, take God's hand, and fight for our dreams, believing that they always arrive at the right moment.

'Let's go,' said the Magus. And Brida could see that this time he was serious.

She made a point of paying the bill; after all, she was the King of the Night. They put on their coats and went out into the cold, which was now less bitter – in a matter of weeks, it would be spring.

They walked together to the bus station. A bus was due to leave in a few minutes. Out in the cold, Brida's feelings of irritation were replaced by a terrible confusion, which she could not explain. She didn't want to get on that bus; everything was wrong; it seemed to her that she'd entirely failed to achieve her main objective of the evening and that she needed to put everything right before she left. She had come there to thank him, and yet she was behaving just as she had on the previous two occasions.

She didn't get on the bus, saying that she felt sick.

Fifteen minutes passed, and another bus arrived.

'I don't want to leave,' she said, 'not because I drank too much and feel ill, but because I've spoiled everything. I haven't thanked you as I should have.'

'This is the last bus,' said the Magus.

'I'll get a taxi later, even if it's expensive.'

When the bus left, Brida regretted not having got on it. She was confused. She had no idea what she wanted. 'I'm drunk,' she thought, and said:

'Let's go for a walk. I need to sober up.'

They strolled through the empty village, with the streetlamps lit and all the windows dark. 'It's just not possible. I saw the light in Lorens' eyes and yet I want to stay here with this man.'

She was just an ordinary, fickle woman, unworthy of all that she had learned and experienced through witchcraft. She was ashamed of herself: all it took was a few glasses of wine, and Lorens – her Soulmate – and everything she'd learned in the Tradition of the Moon were suddenly of no importance. She wondered briefly if she'd been wrong, perhaps the light in Lorens' eyes wasn't the light spoken of in the Tradition of the Sun. But, no, she was merely fooling herself; no one can fail to recognise the light in the eyes of their Soulmate.

If she were to meet Lorens in a crowded theatre, without ever having spoken to him before, the moment their eyes met, she would know for sure that he was the man for her. She would find a way of approaching him, and he would welcome her approaches, because the Traditions are never wrong: Soulmates always find each other in the end. Long before she knew anything about Soulmates, she had often heard people speak about that inexplicable phenomenon: Love at First Sight.

Any human being could recognise that light, without any need for magical powers. She had known about it before she knew of its existence. She had seen it, for example, in the Magus's eyes, the first time they went to the pub together.

She stopped.

'I'm drunk,' she thought again. She must simply forget all about it. She needed to count her money to see if she had enough for a taxi fare back. That was important.

But she had seen the light in the Magus's eyes, the light that showed he was her Soulmate.

'You're very pale,' said the Magus. 'You must have drunk too much.'

'It will pass. Let's sit down for a while until it does. Then I'll go home.'

They sat on a bench while she fumbled around in her bag in search of money. She could stand up, find a taxi and leave forever; she had a Teacher and she knew how to continue her path. She knew her Soulmate too; if she decided to get up now and leave, she would still be fulfilling the mission God had set her.

She might only be twenty-one, but she already knew it was possible to encounter two Soulmates in the same incarnation, and that the result was bound to be pain and suffering.

How could she avoid that?

'I'm not going home,' she said. 'I'm staying here.'

The Magus's eyes shone, and what had been only a hope became a certainty.

They continued walking. The Magus watched Brida's aura change colour many times and hoped she was taking the right path. He understood the storms and earthquakes shaking the soul of his Soulmate, but knew that this was in the nature of transformations. That's how the earth and the stars and mankind are transformed.

They left the village and were walking out into the countryside, towards the mountains where they always met, when Brida asked him to stop.

'Let's go this way,' she said, turning down a path that led into a wheatfield, although why she didn't know. She simply felt a sudden need to feel the force of nature and the friendly spirits who, ever since the world was created, have inhabited all the lovely places of the planet. A huge moon was shining in the sky, illuminating the path and the countryside around.

Without a word, the Magus followed. Deep in his heart, he thanked God for having believed and for not allowing him to make the same mistake again, as he had been on the point of doing just a minute before his prayers were answered.

They walked through the wheatfield, which was transformed by the moonlight into a silver sea. Brida was walking aimlessly, with no idea what her next step would be. A voice inside her was telling her that she should go forward, that she was just as strong as her forebears, and that there was no need to worry, because they were there guiding her steps and protecting her with the Wisdom of Time.

They stopped in the middle of the field. They were surrounded by mountains, and on one of those mountains was a rock from which one could get a fine view of the sunset; there was a hunters' cabin too, higher up than all the others, and a place where, one night, a young woman had confronted fear and darkness.

'I'm ready,' she thought to herself. 'I'm ready and I know I'm protected.' She conjured up the image of the candle at home always burning, her seal with the Tradition of the Moon.

'Here's a good place,' she said, stopping.

She picked up a twig and traced a large circle in the earth while she recited the sacred names her Teacher had taught her. She didn't have her ritual dagger with her, she had none of her sacred objects, but her ancestors were there, and they were telling her that, in order not to be burned at the stake, they had consecrated their kitchen utensils.

'Everything in this world is sacred,' she said. That twig was sacred.

'Yes,' responded the Magus. 'Everything in this world is sacred, and a grain of sand can be a bridge to the invisible.'

'At this moment, though, the bridge to the invisible is my Soulmate,' Brida said.

His eyes filled with tears. God was just.

The two of them entered the circle and she ritually closed it. This was the protective gesture that magi and witches had used since time immemorial.

'You were generous enough to show me your world,' said Brida. 'I perform this ritual now to show that I belong to that world.'

She raised her arms to the moon and invoked the magical forces of nature. She had often seen her Teacher do this when they went to the wood, but now she was doing it, confident that nothing would go wrong. The forces were telling her that she did not need to learn anything; she had only to remember the many times she had done this in her many lives as a witch. She prayed then that the harvest would be good, and that the field would always be fertile. There she was, the priestess who, in other ages, had brought together the earth's knowledge and the transformation of the seed, and had prayed while her man was working the land.

The Magus let Brida take the initial steps. He knew that, at a certain point, he would have to take control, but he needed to leave recorded on space and time the fact that she had begun the process. His Teacher, who, at that moment, was wandering some astral plane awaiting his next life, was there in that field of wheat, just as he had been there in the pub, during his last temptation, and he was doubtless happy that his student had learned from his suffering. The Magus listened in silence to Brida's invocations. When she stopped, she said:

'I don't know why I have done all this, but I know I have done my part.'

'I'll continue,' he said.

Then he turned to the north and imitated the cries of birds that existed now only in myths and legends. That was the only detail that had been lacking. Wicca was a good Teacher and had taught Brida almost everything, apart from the ending.

When the sound of the sacred pelican and the phoenix had been invoked, the whole circle filled with light, a mysterious light, which illuminated nothing around it, but which was, nonetheless, a light. The Magus looked at his Soulmate and there she was, resplendent in her eternal body, with a golden aura and filaments of light emerging from her navel and her head. He knew that she was seeing the same thing, as well as the point of light above his left shoulder, slightly blurred perhaps because of the wine they'd drunk earlier.

'My Soulmate,' she said softly, when she saw the point of light.

'I am going to walk with you through the Tradition of the Moon,' said the Magus. And at once the wheatfield around them became a grey desert, in which there was a temple with women all in white dancing before the temple's vast door. Brida and the Magus were watching this from high up on a dune, and she didn't know if the people could see her.

She felt the Magus's presence beside her and wanted to ask him what the vision meant, but she could not speak. He saw the fear in her eyes, and they returned to the circle of light in the wheatfield.

'What was that?' she asked.

'A present from me to you. That is one of the eleven secret temples of the Tradition of the Moon. A gift of love and gratitude for the fact that you exist and because I have waited so long to find you.'

'Take me with you,' she said. 'Show me how to walk through your world.'

And together they travelled through time and space, through the two Traditions. Brida saw meadows full of flowers, animals she had only read about in books, mysterious castles and cities that seemed to float on clouds of light. The sky lit up as the Magus drew for her, above the wheatfield, the sacred symbols of the Tradition. At one point, they appeared to be in the icy landscape of one of the Earth's two poles, but it was not our planet: other smaller creatures, with long fingers and strange eyes were working on a vast spaceship. Whenever she was about to say something to him, the images would vanish to be replaced by others. Brida understood with her woman's soul that the man by her side was trying to show her everything he had learned over the years, and that he must have been waiting all this time simply to present her with this gift. He could give himself to her now without fear, because she was his Soulmate. She could travel with him through the Elysian Fields, where the enlightened souls live, and which are visited now and then by other souls still in search of enlightenment so that they can nourish themselves with hope.

She could not have said how much time had passed before she found herself back with that luminous being inside the circle she herself had drawn. She had known love before, but until that night love had also meant fear. That fear, however slight, was always a veil; you could see almost everything through it, but not the colours. And at that moment, with her Soulmate there before her, she understood that love was a feeling completely bound up with colour, like thousands of rainbows superimposed one on top of the other.

'How much I missed simply because I was afraid of missing it,' she thought, gazing at those rainbows.

She was lying down, and the luminous being was on top of her, with a point of light above his left shoulder and filaments of light pouring forth from his head and his navel.

'I wanted to speak to you, but I couldn't,' she said.

'That was because of the wine,' he replied.

The pub, the wine and the feeling of irritation were now but a distant memory to Brida.

'Thank you for the visions.'

'They weren't visions,' said the luminous being. 'What you saw was the wisdom of the Earth and of a distant planet.'

Brida didn't want to talk about that. She didn't want any lessons. She wanted only what she had experienced.

'Am I full of light too?'

'Yes, just as I am. The same colour, the same light and the same beams of energy.'

The colour was golden now, and the waves of energy emerging from navel and head were a brilliant pale blue.

'I feel that we were lost and now are saved,' said Brida.

'I'm tired. We should go back. I had a lot to drink too.'

Brida knew that somewhere there existed a world of pubs, wheatfields and bus stations, but she didn't want to go back there; all she wanted was to stay in that field forever. She heard a distant voice making invocations, while the light around her gradually faded, then vanished completely. An enormous moon lit up the sky, illuminating the countryside. They were naked and in each other's arms. And they felt neither cold nor shame.

The Magus asked Brida to close the ritual, since she had begun it. Brida pronounced the words she knew, and he helped where necessary. When the last formulae had been spoken, he opened the magic circle. They got dressed and sat down on the ground.

'Let's leave this place,' said Brida after a while. The Magus got up and she followed. She didn't know what to say; she felt awkward and so did he. They had confessed their love to each other and now, like any other couple in those circumstances, they were embarrassed to look each other in the eye.

Then the Magus broke the silence.

'You must go back to Dublin. I know the number of a taxi firm.'

Brida didn't know whether to feel disappointed or relieved. The feeling of joy was giving way to nausea and a throbbing head. She was sure that she would make very bad company.

'Fine,' she said.

They turned and walked back to the village. He phoned for a taxi from a telephone box. Then they sat on the kerb, waiting for the cab to arrive.

'I want to thank you for tonight,' she said.

He said nothing.

'I don't know if the Equinox festival is just for witches, but it will be a very important day for me.'

'A party is a party.'

'Then I would like to invite you.'

He made a gesture as if wanting to change the subject. He must have been thinking the same thing she was: how hard it was to leave your Soulmate once you'd found them. She imagined him going home alone, wondering when she would come back. She would come back, because her heart was telling her to, but the solitude of forests is harder to bear than the solitude of towns.

'I don't know if love appears suddenly,' Brida went on, 'but I know that I'm open to love, ready for love.'

The taxi came. Brida looked again at the Magus and felt that he had grown many years younger.

'I'm ready for love too,' he said.

The sunlight poured into the spacious kitchen through the sparkling clean windows.

'Did you sleep well, love?'

Her mother put a mug of tea down on the table, along with some toast. Then she went back to the cooker, where she was frying eggs and bacon.

'Yes, I did, thanks. By the way, is my dress ready? I need it for the party the day after tomorrow.'

Her mother brought her the eggs and bacon and sat down. She knew that something odd was going on with her daughter, but could do nothing about it. She would like to talk to her today as she never had before, but she would achieve little if she did. There was a new world out there, a world she didn't know.

She was afraid for her daughter because she loved her and because Brida was alone in that new world.

'My dress will be ready, won't it, Mum?'

'Yes, by lunchtime,' her mother replied. And that made her

happy. At least some things in the world hadn't changed. There were certain problems that mothers continued to solve for their daughters.

She hesitated, then asked:

'How's Lorens?'

'Fine. He's coming to pick me up tomorrow evening.'

She felt simultaneously relieved and sad. Problems of the heart always bruised the soul, and she thanked God that her daughter had no such problems. On the other hand, that was perhaps the one area on which she could advise her, love having changed little over the centuries.

They set off for a walk around the little village where Brida had spent her childhood. The houses had remained unchanged and people were still doing the same things they always had. Her daughter met a few old school friends, who now worked either at the village's one bank or at the stationer's. They said hello and stopped to chat. Some said how Brida had grown, others how pretty she looked. Around ten o'clock they dropped in at the café her mother used to go to on Saturdays, before she met her husband, in the days when she was still hoping to meet someone and be swept up in some whirlwind romance that would put a stop to the endless identical days.

She looked at her daughter again as she told her the latest news about the various people in the village. Brida was still interested, and this pleased her.

'I really do have to have the dress today,' Brida said. She seemed worried, but that couldn't be the reason. She knew that her mother would never let her down.

Her mother decided to take a risk and ask the kind of question children always hate, because they're independent, free and capable of solving their own problems.

'Is anything worrying you?'

'Have you ever been in love with two men at once, Mum?' There was a defiant note in her voice, as if life had set its traps only for her.

Her mother took a bite of her cake. A distant look came into her eyes, as she went off in search of a time that was almost lost.

'Yes, I have.'

Brida stared at her in amazement.

Her mother smiled and invited her to continue their walk.

'Your father was my first and greatest love,' she said, once they'd left the café. 'And I'm still very happy with him. When I was younger than you are now, I had everything I could have dreamed of. At the time, my friends and I believed that love was the only reason for living. If you failed to find someone, then you could never claim to have realised your dreams.'

'Stick to the point, Mum.' Brida was impatient.

'I had other dreams too, though. I dreamed, for example, of doing what you did, going off to the big city and discovering the world that lay beyond my village. The only way I could get my parents to accept my decision was by telling them that I needed to follow some course of study that wasn't available locally.

'The sleepless nights I spent, thinking about how to broach the subject with them. I planned exactly what I was going to say and what they would say in reply and how I would answer.'

Her mother had never spoken to her like this before. Brida felt a mixture of affection and regret. They could have enjoyed other such moments, but they were both too caught up in their own worlds and their own values.

'Two days before I was going to talk to my parents, I met your father. I looked into his eyes and saw a special light there, as if I'd met the person I most wanted to meet in the world.'

'Yes, I've had the same experience.'

'After I met your father, I realised, too, that my search was over. I didn't need any other explanation of the world. I didn't feel frustrated to be living here, always seeing the same people and doing the same things. Every day was different, because of the great love between us.

'We started going out together and then we got married. I never talked to him about my dreams of going to live in a big city, of discovering other places and other people. Because suddenly, the whole world fitted into my village. Love became my explanation for life.'

'You mentioned someone else, Mum.'

'Let me show you something,' her mother said in reply.

They walked to the bottom of the steps that led up to the Catholic church in the village, and which had been destroyed and then rebuilt over the centuries. Brida used to go to mass there every Sunday and she remembered that, as a child, climbing those steps had been really hard. At the beginning of each stretch of balustrade was the carving of a saint – St Paul to the left and St James to the right – rather worn by time and by tourists. The ground was covered in dry leaves, as if autumn were about to arrive, not spring.

The church was at the top of the hill, and it was impossible to see it from where they were because of the trees. Her mother sat down on the first step and invited Brida to do the same.

'This is where it happened,' she said. 'One afternoon, for some reason or other, I decided to come here to pray. I needed to be alone, to think about my life, and I thought the church would be a good place to do so.

'When I got here, however, I met a man. He was sitting where you are now, with two suitcases beside him, and he looked totally lost, desperately leafing through the book he was holding. I thought he must be a tourist in search of a hotel and so I went over to him. I even started talking to him. He seemed a bit startled at first, but then he relaxed.

'He said that he wasn't lost. He was an archaeologist and had been driving north – where some ruins had been found – when the engine packed up. A mechanic would arrive soon, and so he'd decided to visit the church while he waited. He asked me about the village and the other villages nearby, about historic monuments.

'Suddenly, all the problems I'd been grappling with disappeared as if by magic. I felt really useful and started telling him everything I knew, feeling that the many years I'd spent in the region at last had some meaning. Before me was a man who had studied peoples and societies, who might hold in his memory, for the benefit of future generations, everything I'd heard or discovered when I was a child. That man sitting on the steps made me understand that I was important to the world and to the history of my country. I felt necessary, and that's the best feeling a human being can have.

'When I'd finished telling him about the church, we went on to talk about other things. I told him how proud I was of my village, and he responded with some words by a writer whose name I don't recall now, something about how understanding your own village helps you understand the world.'

'Tolstoy,' said Brida.

But her mother was still travelling in time, just as she herself had done one day, except that her mother didn't require cathedrals adrift in space, subterranean libraries, or dusty books; she needed only the memory of that spring afternoon and a man sitting on the steps with his suitcases.

'We talked for quite a while. I had the whole afternoon free to spend with him, but since the mechanic might arrive at any moment, I decided to make the most of every second. I asked him about his world, about excavations, about the challenges of spending his life looking for the past in the present. He spoke to me of the warriors, wise men and pirates who had once inhabited our country.

'Before I knew it, the sun was low on the horizon, and never, in all my life, had time passed so quickly. I sensed that he felt the same. He kept asking me questions to keep the conversation going, not giving me time to say that I had to leave. He talked non-stop, telling me all about his experiences, and he wanted to know everything about me too. I could see in his eyes that he desired me, even though, at the time, I was nearly twice the age you are now.

'It was spring, there was a lovely smell of new things in the air, and I felt young again. There's a flower that only blooms in the autumn; well, that afternoon, I felt like that flower. As if, suddenly, in the autumn of my life, when I thought I'd experienced everything I could experience, that man had appeared on the steps purely to show me that feelings – love, for example – do not grow old along with the body. Feelings form part of a world I don't know, but it's a world where there's no time, no space, no frontiers.'

She remained silent for a while. Her eyes were still far-off, fixed on that distant spring.

'There was I, like a 38-year-old adolescent, feeling that someone desired me. He didn't want me to leave. Then all of a sudden, he stopped talking. He looked deep into my eyes and smiled. It was as if he'd understood with his heart what I was thinking, and wanted to tell me that it was true, that I *was* very important to him. For some time, we said nothing, and then we said goodbye. The mechanic had still not arrived.

'For many days, I wondered if that man really had existed, or if he was an angel sent by God to teach me the secret lessons of life. In the end, I decided that he had been a real man, a man who had loved me, even if only for an afternoon, and during that afternoon, he'd given me everything he had kept to himself throughout his whole life: his struggles, his joys, his difficulties and his dreams. That afternoon I gave myself wholly as well – I was his companion, his wife, his audience, his lover. In a matter of only a few hours, I experienced the love of a lifetime.'

* * *

Mother looked at daughter. She hoped her daughter had understood, but deep down, she felt that Brida lived in a world in which that kind of love had no place.

'I've never stopped loving your father, not for a single day,' she concluded. 'He's always been by my side, doing his best, and I want to be with him until the end. But the heart's a mysterious thing, and I still don't really understand what happened that afternoon. What I do know is that meeting that man left me feeling more confident, and showed me I was still capable of loving and being loved, and it taught me something else that I'll never forget: finding one important thing in your life doesn't mean you have to give up all the other important things.

'I still think of him sometimes. I'd like to know where he is, if he found what he was looking for that afternoon, if he's still alive, or if God took his soul. I know he'll never come back, which is why I could love him with such strength and such certainty, because I would never lose him; he had given himself to me entirely that afternoon.'

Her mother got up.

'I'd better go home and finish making your dress,' she said.

'I think I'll stay here for a while,' Brida replied.

She went over to her daughter and kissed her fondly.

'Thank you for listening to me. It's the first time I've ever told anyone that story. I was always afraid I might die without having done so, and that it would be wiped forever from the face of the Earth. Now you will keep it for me.'

Brida went up the steps and stood outside the church. This small, round building was the pride of the region. It was one of the first places of Christian worship in Ireland, and every year, scholars and tourists came to visit it. Nothing remained of the original fifth-century structure, apart from some fragments of floor; each destruction, however, had left some part intact and so the visitor could trace the history of the various architectural styles that made up the church.

Inside, an organ was playing, and Brida stood outside for a while, listening to the music. Everything was so clearly laid out in that church; the universe was exactly where it should be, and anyone coming in through its doors had no need to worry about anything. There were no mysterious forces far above, no Dark Nights that called on one to believe without understanding. There was no more talk of burning people at the stake, and the religions of the world lived together as if they were allies, binding man once more to God. Her island was still an exception to that peaceful co-existence – in the North, people still killed each other in the name of religion, but that would eventually end. God had almost been explained away: He was our generous Father, and we were all saved.

'I'm a witch,' she said to herself, struggling against a growing impulse to enter the church. Hers was now a different Tradition, and even if it was the same God, if she walked through those doors she would be profaning the place, and would, in turn, be profaned.

She lit a cigarette and stared across at the horizon, trying not to think about these things. She thought, instead, of her mother. She felt like running back home, flinging her arms about her neck, and telling her that in two days' time she was going to be initiated into the Great Mysteries of witchcraft, that she had made journeys in time, that she had experienced the power of sex, that she could guess what was in a shop window using only the techniques of the Tradition of the Moon. She needed love and understanding, because she, too, knew stories she could tell no one.

The organ stopped playing, and Brida once again heard the voices of the village, the singing of the birds, the wind stirring the branches and announcing the coming of spring. At the back of the church, a door opened and closed. Someone had left. For a moment, she saw herself on a Sunday in her childhood, standing where she was now, feeling irritated because the mass was so long and Sunday was the only day when she was free to explore the fields.

'I must go in.' Perhaps her mother would understand what she was feeling, but at that moment, she was far away. There before her was an empty church. She had never asked Wicca precisely what Christianity's role had been in everything that happened. She had a sense that if she walked through that door, she would be betraying all her sisters who had been burned at the stake.

'But then I was burned at the stake too,' she said to herself. She remembered the prayer Wicca had said on the day commemorating the martyrdom of the witches. And in that prayer, she had mentioned Jesus and the Virgin Mary. Love was above everything else, and there was no hatred in love, only the occasional mistake. At one point, men may have decided to make themselves God's representatives and subsequently made mistakes, but God had nothing to do with that.

When she did finally go in, there was no one else inside. A few lit candles showed that someone had taken the trouble that morning to renew their alliance with a force they could only sense, and in that way had crossed the bridge between the visible and the invisible. She regretted her thoughts before entering the church: nothing was explained here either, and people had to take a chance and plunge into the Dark Night of Faith. Before her, arms outspread, was that seemingly simple God.

He could not help her. She was alone with her decisions, and no one could help her. She needed to learn to take risks. She didn't have the same advantages as the crucified man before her, who had known what his mission was, because he was the son of God. He had never made a mistake. He had never known ordinary human love, only love for his Father. All he needed to do was to reveal his wisdom and teach humankind the true path to heaven.

But was that all? She remembered a Sunday catechism class, when the priest had been more inspired than usual. They'd been studying the episode when Jesus, sweating blood, was praying to God and asking Him to remove the cup from which he was being forced to drink.

'But why, if he already knew he was the son of God?' asked the priest. 'Because he only knew it with his heart. If he was absolutely sure, his mission would be meaningless, because he would not be entirely human. Being human means having doubts and yet still continuing on your path.'

She looked again at the image, and for the first time in her entire life, felt closer to it. There perhaps was a man, frightened and alone, facing death and asking: 'Father, Father, why hast thou forsaken me?' If he said that, it was because even he wasn't sure where he was going. He had taken a chance and plunged, as all men do, into the Dark Night, knowing that he would only find the answer at the end of his journey. He, too, had to go through the anxiety of making decisions, of leaving his father and mother and his little village to go in search of the secrets of men and the mysteries of the Law.

If he had been through all that, then he must have known love, even though the Gospels never mention this – love between people is much more difficult to understand than love for a Supreme Being. But now she remembered that, when he had risen again, the first person to whom he appeared was a woman, who had accompanied him to the last.

The silent image appeared to agree with her. He had known people, wine, bread, parties and all the beauties of the world. It was impossible that he had not also known the love of a woman, which is why he had sweated blood on the Mount of Olives, because, having known the love of one person, it was very hard to leave the Earth and to sacrifice himself for the love of all men.

He had experienced everything the world could offer and yet he continued on his journey, knowing that the Dark Night could end on the cross or on the pyre.

'Lord, we're all in the world to run the risks of that Dark Night. I'm afraid of death, but even more afraid of wasting my life. I'm afraid of love, because it involves things that are beyond our understanding; it sheds such a brilliant light, but the shadow it casts frightens me.'

She suddenly realised that she was praying. That silent, simple God was looking at her, apparently understanding her words and taking them seriously.

For a while, she sat waiting for a response from him, but heard not a sound and saw not a sign. The answer was there before her, in that man nailed to the cross. He had played his part, and shown to the world that, if everyone played their part, no one else would have to suffer, because he had suffered for all those who'd had the courage to fight for their dreams.

Brida found herself quietly weeping, although she didn't quite know why.

The day was overcast, but it wasn't going to rain. Lorens had lived in that city for many years and knew its clouds. He got up and went into the kitchen to make some coffee. Brida joined him just as the water was boiling.

'You came to bed very late last night,' he said.

She didn't answer.

'Today's the day,' he went on, 'and I know how important it is to you. I would love to be there with you.'

'It's a party,' said Brida.

'What does that mean?'

'It's a party, and for as long as we've known each other, we've always gone to parties together. You're invited too.'

The Magus went out to see if the previous day's rain had damaged the bromeliads in his garden. They were fine, and he smiled to himself; it seemed that the forces of nature did sometimes collaborate.

He thought about Wicca. She wouldn't be able to see the points of light, because they were visible only to the respective Soulmates, but she was sure to notice the energy from the rays of light moving between him and her student. Witches were, above all else, women.

The Tradition of the Moon described this as the 'Vision of Love', and although it was something that could happen between people who were not each other's Soulmate, but merely in love, he imagined that it would, nevertheless, fill her with anger, female anger, the kind felt by Snow White's stepmother, who could not allow another woman to be more beautiful than her.

Wicca, however, was a Teacher and would immediately realise how absurd such feelings of anger were, but, by then, her aura would already have changed colour.

He would go over to her then, kiss her on the cheek and say that he could see she was jealous. She would deny this, and he would ask why she was angry.

She would say that she was a woman and didn't need to explain her feelings. He would give her another kiss on the cheek, because what she said was true. And he would tell her how much he'd missed her during the time they'd been apart, and that he still admired her more than any other woman in the world, with the exception of Brida, because Brida was his Soulmate.

Wicca, being a wise woman, would feel happy then.

'I must be getting old,' he thought. 'I'm starting to imagine conversations.' Then it occurred to him that it wasn't just a matter of age; that was how men in love had always behaved.

icca was pleased because the rain had stopped and the clouds would clear before nightfall. Nature needed to be in accord with the works of human beings.

She had taken all the necessary steps; everyone had played their part; everything was in place.

She went over to the altar and invoked her Teacher. She asked him to be present that night. Three new witches were to be initiated into the Great Mysteries, and she had sole responsibility for their initiation.

Then she went into the kitchen to make some coffee. She squeezed some orange juice and ate some toast and a few crispbreads. She still took care of her appearance, because she knew how pretty she was. She didn't need to neglect her beauty in order to prove that she was also intelligent and capable.

While she distractedly stirred her coffee, she remembered a day just like this many years before, when her Teacher had sealed her destiny with the Great Mysteries. For a moment, she tried to imagine the person she had been then, what her dreams had been, what she'd wanted from life.

'I must be getting old,' she said out loud, 'sitting here, thinking about the past.' She drank her coffee and began her preparations. There were still things to do. She knew, though, that she wasn't getting old. In her world, Time did not exist.

*B*rida was surprised by the number of cars parked by the roadside. That morning's heavy clouds had been replaced by a clear sky from which the last rays of the setting sun were now fading. Despite the distinct chill in the air, it was still the first day of spring.

She invoked the protection of the spirits of the forest, and then looked at Lorens. He rather awkwardly repeated the same words, and yet he seemed quite happy to be there. If they were to remain together, they would each, from time to time, have to enter the other's reality. Between them, too, there existed a bridge between the visible and the invisible. Magic was present in their every act.

They walked quickly through the wood and soon reached the clearing. Brida was prepared now for what she saw: men and women of all ages, and doubtless from a wide range of professions, were gathered in groups, talking and trying to make the whole event seem like the most natural thing in the world. In reality, though, they were feeling as perplexed as she and Lorens.

'Are all these people part of the ceremony?' Lorens asked, for he hadn't been expecting such a crowd.

Brida explained that some, like him, were guests. She didn't know exactly who would be taking part, but all would be revealed at the chosen moment.

They selected a corner to put their things down, including the bag Lorens was carrying. Inside were Brida's dress and three bottles of wine. Wicca had recommended that each person, both participants and guests, should bring a large bottle of wine. Before they left the house, Lorens had asked who the other guest was. Brida told him that it was the Magus whom she went to visit in the mountains, and Lorens gave the matter no further thought.

'Imagine,' he heard a woman next to him comment, 'imagine what my friends would say if they knew I was at a real witches' Sabbath.'

A witches' Sabbath. The celebration that had survived the spilled blood, the fires, the Age of Reason and oblivion. Lorens tried to reassure himself; after all, there were many other people like him there. However, a shudder ran through him when he saw a pile of logs in the middle of the clearing.

Wicca was talking to some other people, but as soon as she saw Brida, she came over to say hello and to ask if she was all right. Brida thanked her for her kindness and introduced Lorens.

'And I've invited someone else as well,' she said.

Wicca looked at her, surprised, then smiled broadly. Brida was sure she knew who she meant.

'I'm glad,' Wicca said. 'After all, it's his celebration too. And it's ages since I saw that old wizard. Maybe he's learned a thing or two.'

More people arrived, and Brida couldn't tell who were the guests and who were the participants. Half an hour later, when almost a hundred people were gathered in the clearing, talking quietly, Wicca called for silence.

'This is a ceremony,' she said, 'but it is also a celebration. And no celebration can begin without everyone filling their glass.'

She opened her bottle of wine and filled the glass of the person next to her. The wine was soon flowing freely, and the voices grew louder. Brida didn't want to drink. Still fresh in her memory was a field of wheat in which a man had shown her the secret temples of the Tradition of the Moon. Besides, the guest she was expecting had still not arrived.

Lorens, on the other hand, was starting to feel much more relaxed and had started chatting to the people around him.

'It really is a party!' he said to Brida, smiling. He had come there expecting something extraordinary, but it turned out it was just a party, and much more fun than the parties held by his fellow scientists.

A little way off stood a man with a white beard, whom he recognised as a professor from the university. He didn't know quite what to do, but, after a while, the professor recognised him too and raised his glass in greeting.

Lorens felt relieved. Witches were no longer hunted, nor were their sympathisers.

'It's like a picnic,' Brida heard someone say. Yes, it was like a picnic and that made her feel rather irritated. She had expected something more ritualistic, more like the Sabbaths that had inspired Goya, Saint-Saëns and Picasso. She picked up the bottle beside her and began to drink.

A party. Crossing the bridge between the visible and the invisible by means of a party. Brida was intrigued to know how anything sacred could possibly happen in such a secular atmosphere.

Night was falling fast, and people continued to drink. Just as darkness threatened to submerge everything, some of the men present – without performing any specific ritual – lit the fire. That is how it had been in the past. Before fire became a powerful element in the rituals of witchcraft, it had been merely a source of light. A light around which women gathered to talk about their men, their magical experiences, their encounters with incubi and succubi, the much-feared sexual demons of the Middle Ages. That is how it had been in the past – a party, a huge popular festival, a joyful celebration of spring and hope, in an age when being happy was a challenge to the Law, because no one could enjoy themselves in a world made only to tempt the weak. The lords of the land, shut up in their dark castles, gazed out at the fires in the forests and felt as if they'd been robbed – those peasants were eager for happiness, and no one who has experienced happiness can ever again feel at ease with sadness. The peasants might then expect to be happy all year round, and that would threaten the whole political and religious system.

Four or five people, who were already slightly tipsy, began dancing round the fire, perhaps in imitation of a witches' Sabbath. Amongst the dancers Brida saw an Initiate whom she'd met when Wicca commemorated the martyrdom of the sisters. She was shocked. She had assumed followers of the

Tradition of the Moon would behave in a way more in keeping with that sacred place. She remembered the night she had spent with the Magus, and how drink had hindered communication between them during their astral travel.

'My friends will be green with envy,' she heard someone say. 'They'll never believe I was here.'

That was too much. She needed to get a little distance, to understand properly what was going on, and to resist a strong desire simply to leave and go home before she became entirely disillusioned with everything she'd believed in for nearly a year now. She looked for Wicca, and saw her talking and laughing with some of the guests. The number of people dancing round the fire was growing larger all the time; some were clapping and singing, accompanied by others keeping time by beating on the empty bottles with sticks or keys.

'I need to go for a walk,' she told Lorens.

A group of people had gathered round him, fascinated by what he was telling them about ancient stars and the miracles of modern physics. However, he immediately stopped talking and asked:

'Would you like me to come with you?'

'No, I'd rather be alone.'

She left the group and headed off into the forest. The voices were growing ever louder and more raucous, and everything – the drunkenness, the comments, the people playing at being witches and wizards around the fire – became mixed up in her head. She had waited so long for this night, but it was turning out to be just another party, like one of those charity dos, where people eat, get drunk, tell jokes, and then make speeches about the need to help the Indians in the Southern Hemisphere or the seals at the North Pole.

She began walking through the forest, always keeping within sight of the fire. She walked along a path that gave her a view from above the central stone. However, seen from high up, the view was even more disappointing: Wicca was busy circulating among the different groups, asking if everything was all right; people were dancing round the fire; a few couples were already exchanging their first drunken kisses. Lorens was talking animatedly to two men, perhaps about things that would have been fine in the setting of a bar, but not at a celebration like this. A latecomer entered the wood, a stranger attracted by the noise, in search of a little fun.

She recognised his way of walking.

The Magus.

Startled, Brida began running back down the path. She wanted to reach him before he got to the party. She needed him to help her, as he had before. She needed to understand the meaning of what was going on there.

Wicca certainly knows how to organise a Sabbath,' thought the Magus as he approached. He could see and feel the free flow of energy among the people present. At this phase of the ritual, the Sabbath resembled any other party; it was important to ensure that all the guests were on the same wavelength. At his first Sabbath, he had felt very shocked by all this. He remembered calling his Teacher over and asking him what was going on.

'Haven't you ever been to a party before?' his Teacher had asked, annoyed at the Magus for interrupting an interesting conversation.

Of course he had, the Magus said.

'And what makes for a good party?'

'Everyone enjoying themselves.'

'Men have been holding parties since the days when they lived in caves,' said his Teacher. 'They're the first group rituals we know of, and the Tradition of the Sun took it upon itself to keep that ritual alive. A good party cleanses the minds of all those taking part, but it's very difficult to make that happen; it only takes a few people to spoil the general mood. Those people think they're more important than the others; they're hard to please; they think they're wasting their time because they can't make contact with anyone else. And they usually end up the victims of a mysterious form of poetic justice: they tend to leave weighed down by the astral larvae given off by those people who *have* managed to bond with others. Remember, the first road to God is prayer, the second is joy.'

Many years had passed since that conversation with his Teacher. The Magus had taken part in many Sabbaths since then, and he knew that this was a very skilfully arranged example; the collective energy level was growing all the time.

He looked for Brida. There were a lot of people there, and he wasn't used to crowds. He knew that he needed to partake of that collective energy, and he was quite prepared to do so, but first he needed to re-accustom himself. She could help him. He would feel more at ease once he had found her.

He was a Magus. He knew about the point of light. All he needed was to alter his state of consciousness and the point of light would appear in the midst of all those people. For years, he had searched for that light, and now it was there only yards away from him.

The Magus altered his state of consciousness. He looked again at the people gathered there, this time with a changed perception, and he could see a vast range of different-coloured auras; all of them, though, were shifting closer to the colour that would predominate that night.

'Wicca really is an excellent Teacher,' he thought again. 'She works very fast.' Soon all the auras, the energy vibrations that surround each physical body, would be vibrating as one. And then the second part of the ritual could begin.

He looked to left and right and finally located the point of light. He decided to surprise her and approached without a sound.

'Brida,' he said.

His Soulmate turned round.

'She's gone for a walk,' a young man said politely.

For a moment that seemed to last for ever, the Magus looked at the man standing before him.

'You must be the Magus that Brida has told me so much about,' said Lorens. 'Join us. She won't be long.'

But Brida was already there. She was standing opposite the two men, breathing hard, eyes wide.

From the other side of the fire, the Magus sensed someone watching. He knew that look; it would not be able to see the points of light, because only Soulmates could recognise each other, but it was a deep and ancient look, one that knew the Tradition of the Moon, and the hearts of men and women.

The Magus turned and faced Wicca. She smiled at him from the other side of the fire – in a fraction of a second she had understood everything.

Brida also had her eyes fixed on the Magus. They were alight with pleasure. He had come.

'I'd like to introduce you to Lorens,' she said. The party

suddenly seemed like fun, and she no longer needed any explanations.

The Magus was still in that altered state of consciousness. He saw Brida's aura rapidly changing and moving towards the colour that Wicca had chosen. She was pleased and happy that he had come, and anything he said or did could so easily ruin her Initiation that night. He must, at all costs, control his feelings.

'Pleased to meet you,' he said to Lorens. 'How about pouring me a glass of wine?'

Lorens smiled and held out the bottle.

'Welcome to the group,' he said. 'I'm sure you'll enjoy the party.'

Wicca looked away and gave a sigh of relief. Brida had noticed nothing. She was a good student, and Wicca would have been loth to remove her from that night's initiation ceremony because she had failed to take the simplest step of all, by not joining in with the general good cheer.

'And he can take care of himself.' The Magus had years of work and discipline behind him. He would be capable of keeping his feelings in check, long enough at least to replace those feelings with something else. She respected his hard work and his stubbornness, and felt slightly afraid of his immense power.

She chatted with a few of the other guests, but couldn't quite get over her surprise at what she'd just seen. So that was why he'd paid so much attention to Brida, who was, after all, a witch like any other witch who had spent various incarnations learning the Tradition of the Moon.

Brida was his Soulmate.

'My feminine intuition clearly isn't working very well.' She had imagined everything, except that most obvious of reasons. She consoled herself by thinking that at least the result of all her curiosity had been a positive one: it was the path chosen by God to enable her to rediscover her student.

The Magus spotted someone he knew in the crowd and excused himself for a moment to go and speak to him. Brida was euphoric, enjoying his presence there beside her, but she felt it best to let him leave. Her feminine intuition was telling her that it was best if he and Lorens didn't spend too much time together; they might become friends, and when two men are in love with the same woman, it's better that they hate each other than that they become friends. Because, if that happened, she would end up losing them both.

She looked at the people round the fire, and suddenly she felt like dancing too. She asked Lorens to join her; he hesitated for a second, but then took courage and said 'Yes'. People were still spinning round and clapping, drinking wine and beating out a rhythm on the empty wine bottles with sticks and keys. Whenever she danced past the Magus, he smiled and raised his glass to her. This was one of the best nights of her life.

Wicca joined the circle of dancers, where everyone was feeling relaxed and happy. The guests, who had been rather anxious about what might happen and worried about what they might see, had now entered fully into the spirit of the night. Spring had arrived, and they needed to celebrate, to fill their soul with faith in future sunlit days, and forget as quickly as possible the grey evenings and lonely nights spent at home.

The clapping grew louder, and now it was Wicca setting the rhythm. It was an insistent, regular rhythm. Everyone's eyes were fixed on the fire. No one was cold; it was as if summer had arrived already. The people round the fire began to take off their sweaters.

'Let's sing!' said Wicca. She sang a simple two-verse song several times, and soon everyone was singing with her. A few people recognised it as a witches' mantra where what mattered was the sound of the words, not the meaning. It was the sound of union with the Gifts; and those endowed with magic vision – like the Magus and the other Teachers present – could see the filaments of light joining various people.

Lorens eventually grew bored with the dancing and went to join the 'musicians'. Others moved away from the fire, some because they were tired and others because Wicca had asked them to help keep the rhythm going. Only the Initiates noticed what was happening, that the party was beginning to enter sacred territory. Very soon, the only people dancing round the fire were the women from the Tradition of the Moon and the witches who were to be initiated that night.

Even Wicca's male students stopped dancing; the initiation ritual for the men was different and took place on a different date. What was turning and turning in the astral plane immediately above the fire was female energy, the energy of transformation. So it had been since time immemorial.

Brida began to feel very hot. It couldn't be the wine, because she'd drunk very little. It was probably the flames from the fire. She had a great desire to take off her blouse, but she felt embarrassed, an embarrassment that gradually lost all meaning as she clapped and sang that simple song and danced around the fire. Her eyes were now fixed on the flames, and the world seemed less and less important; it was a feeling very similar to the one she'd experienced when the tarot cards had revealed themselves to her for the first time.

'I'm going into a trance,' she thought. 'But so what? This party's fun!'

'What strange music,' Lorens was thinking, as he kept time, beating the bottle. His ear, trained to listen to his own body, had noticed that the rhythm of the clapping and the sound of the words vibrated exactly in the middle of his chest, as happened when he heard the bass drum in a concert of classical music. The odd thing was that the rhythm also seemed to be dictating the beating of his heart.

As Wicca quickened the pace, his heart beat faster too. The same thing must be happening to everyone.

'More blood is flowing to my brain,' the scientific part of his mind told him. But he was part of a witches' ritual and this was no time to be thinking such things; he could talk to Brida about it later.

'I'm at a party and I want to have fun,' he said out loud. Someone beside him cried: 'Hear, hear!' and Wicca's clapping grew a little faster.

'I'm free. I'm proud of my body because it's the manifestation of God in the visible world.' The heat from the fire was becoming unbearable. The world seemed far away, and she no longer cared about superficial things. She was alive, the blood was coursing through her veins, and she was entirely given over, body and soul, to her search. Dancing round that fire was not new to her, for the rhythm awoke dormant memories of when she had been a Teacher of the Wisdom of Time. She wasn't alone, because that party was a re-encounter with herself and with the Tradition she'd carried through many lives. She felt a profound respect for herself.

She was once again in a body, and it was a beautiful body, one that had fought for millions of years to survive in a hostile world. It had lived in the sea, crawled upon the earth, climbed trees, walked on all fours, and was now proudly standing with its two feet on the ground. That body deserved respect for its long struggle. There were no beautiful or ugly bodies, because all had followed the same trajectory; all were the visible part of the soul they inhabited.

She felt proud, deeply proud of her body.

She took off her blouse.

She wasn't wearing a bra, but that didn't matter. Yes, she was proud of her body, and no one could criticise her for that: even if she were seventy years old, she would still be proud of her body, because it was through her body that the soul could do its work.

The other women around the fire did the same, and that didn't matter either.

She unbuckled the belt on her trousers and finally stood there completely naked. She felt freer than at any other time in her entire life. There was no reason behind what she was doing; she was doing it simply because nakedness was the only way to show how free her soul was at that moment. It didn't matter that other people were there, clothed and watching; all she wished was that they could feel about their bodies as she felt about hers. She could dance freely, and nothing impeded her movements. Every atom of her body was touching the air, and the air was generous; it brought with it, from afar, secrets and perfumes to clothe her from head to toe.

The men and the other guests beating the wine bottles noticed that the women around the fire were naked. They clapped or held hands and sang – sometimes softly and sometimes wildly. No one knew who was setting the rhythm, whether it was the people beating time on the bottles, the clapping, or the music. They all seemed aware of what was happening, but if, at that moment, one of them had been brave enough to break the rhythm, they could not have done so. At this point in the ritual, one of the Teacher's greatest problems was making sure that no one realised they were in a trance. They needed to feel that they were in control, even though they weren't. Wicca was not violating the one Law which, if broken, was punished by the Tradition with exceptional severity – manipulating the free will of others – because everyone there knew they were present at a witches' Sabbath, and, for witches, life means communion with the Universe.

*　*　*

Later, when this night was just a memory, none of these people would tell what they had seen. There was no prohibition on doing so, but they all felt they were in the presence of a powerful force, a mysterious, sacred force; intense and implacable, one that no human being would dare to defy.

'Turn!' said the woman in the black, ankle-length dress. She was the only woman still fully clothed. All the others were naked as they danced and clapped and spun.

A man placed a pile of dresses beside her. Three of them would be worn for the first time, and two were very similar in style. These were people with the same Gift, which took material form in the dress each woman had dreamed.

There was no need for Wicca to clap now, for the others continued to do so as if she were still keeping the beat.

She knelt down, pressed her thumbs to her head and began to work the Power.

The Power of the Tradition of the Moon, the Wisdom of Time, was there. It was a highly dangerous Power, one that witches could only invoke once they had become Teachers. Wicca knew how to use it but, even so, she first asked for her Teacher's protection.

In that power dwelled the Wisdom of Time. There was the Serpent, wise and masterful. Only the Virgin, by crushing the serpent's head beneath her heel, could subjugate it. And so Wicca prayed to the Virgin Mary as well, asking her for purity of soul, steadiness of hand, and the protection of her cloak, so that she could bring down that Power on the women before her, without it seducing or overwhelming any of them.

With her face lifted to the sky, her voice steady and confident, she recited the words of St Paul:

'If any man defile the temple of God, him shall God destroy; for the temple of God is holy, which temple ye are.

'Let no man deceive himself. If any man among you seemeth to be wise in this world, let him become a fool, that he may be wise.

'For the wisdom of this world is foolishness with God. For it is written, He taketh the wise in their own craftiness.

'And again, the Lord knoweth the thoughts of the wise, that they are vain.

'Therefore, let no man glory in men. For all things are yours.'

With a few deft movements of her hand, Wicca slowed the rhythm of the clapping. The people beating on the wine bottles beat more slowly and the women, too, began to spin and turn more slowly. Wicca was keeping the Power under control, and the whole orchestra had to work well, from the loudest horn to the quietest violin. To achieve this, she needed the assistance of the Power, but without actually surrendering to it.

She clapped her hands and made the necessary noises. Gradually, everyone stopped playing and dancing. The witches came over to Wicca and picked up their dresses – only three women remained naked. At that point, there had been an hour and twenty-eight minutes of continuous sound, and although all those present were in a state of altered consciousness, none of them, with the exception of the three naked women, had, for one moment, lost a sense of where they were or what they were doing.

The three naked women, however, were still in a trance. Wicca held out her ritual dagger and directed all its concentrated energy at them.

Their Gifts would soon become apparent. This was their way of serving the world; having walked long and tortuous paths, they had finally arrived. The world had tested them in every possible way, and they were worthy of what they had achieved. In daily life, they would continue to have their customary weaknesses and resentments, perform their usual small acts of kindness and of cruelty. The agony and the ecstasy would continue, as it would for everyone who is part of a world in a constant state of flux. However, at the appointed time, they would learn that each human being carries within them something far more important than their own self, namely, their particular Gift. For God placed in the hands of each and every person a Gift, the instrument He used to reveal Himself to the world and to help humanity. God chose human beings to be His helpers on Earth.

Some came to understand their Gift through the Tradition of the Sun, others through the Tradition of the Moon, but all eventually learned what their Gift was, even if it took several incarnations to do so.

Wicca stood by the great stone placed there by Celtic priests. The witches, in their black robes, formed a semicircle around her.

She looked at the three naked women. Their eyes were shining.

'Come here.'

The women walked into the middle of the semicircle. Wicca then asked them to lie face down on the ground, with their arms outstretched to form a cross.

The Magus watched Brida lie down on the ground. He tried to concentrate only on her aura, but he was a man, and a man always looks at a woman's body.

He didn't want to remember. He didn't want to think about whether he was suffering or not. He was aware of only one thing – that his mission with his Soulmate beside him was over.

'It's a shame to have spent so little time with her.' But he couldn't think like that. Somewhere in Time, they had shared the same body, felt the same pain and been made happy by the same pleasures. Perhaps they had walked together through a forest similar to this and gazed up at the night sky where the same bright stars shone. He smiled at the thought of his Teacher, who had made him spend so long in the forest merely in order that he should understand his encounter with his Soulmate.

That was how things were in the Tradition of the Sun; each person was obliged to learn what he needed to learn and not merely what he wanted to learn. In his man-heart he would weep for a long time, but in his Magus-heart, he felt exultant and grateful to the forest.

Wicca looked at the three women lying at her feet and gave thanks to God that she had been able to continue doing the same work throughout so many lives; the Tradition of the Moon was inexhaustible. The clearing in the wood had been consecrated by Celtic priests in a time now long forgotten, and little remained of their rituals, only perhaps the stone before which she was standing. It was a huge stone, so large it could not possibly have been transported there by human hands, but then the Ancients had known how to move such stones by magical means. They had built pyramids, observatories and whole cities in the mountains of South America, using only the forces known to the Tradition of the Moon. Such knowledge was no longer needed by man, and had been erased from Time so that it could not be turned to destructive ends. Nevertheless, out of pure curiosity, Wicca would like to have known how they had done it.

There were a few Celtic spirits present, and she greeted them. They were teachers who had ceased being reincarnated, and now formed part of Earth's secret government; without them, without the strength of their knowledge, the planet would long since have lost its way. Above the trees to the left of the clearing, these Celtic teachers were hovering in the air, astral bodies surrounded by an intense white light. Through the centuries, they had come there at every Equinox, to make sure that the Tradition was being maintained. Yes, said Wicca with a certain pride, the Equinoxes continued to be celebrated even after all Celtic culture had disappeared from the official History of the World. Because no one can destroy the Tradition of the Moon, only the Hand of God.

She observed the priests for a while longer. What would they make of people today? Did they feel a nostalgia for the days when they used to come to this place and when contact with God seemed simpler and more direct? Wicca thought not, and her instinct was confirmed. The garden of God was being constructed out of human emotions, and for this to happen, people had to live a long time, in different ages, often adopting very different customs. As in the rest of the Universe, man was following his evolutionary path, and each day he was better than on the previous day, even if he forgot the previous day's lessons, even if he complained, claiming that life was unfair.

Because the Kingdom of Heaven is like the seed that a man plants in a field; he sleeps and wakes, day and night, and the seed grows even though he knows not how. These lessons were engraved on the Soul of the World and existed for the benefit of all humanity. It was important that there were still people like those present at the ceremony, people who were not afraid of the Dark Night of the Soul, as wise St John of the Cross had described it. Each step, each act of faith, redeemed the whole human race anew. As long as there were people who knew that, in God's eyes, all of man's wisdom was madness, the world would continue along the path of light.

She felt proud of her pupils, male and female, who had proved capable of sacrificing the comfort of a world of nice, neat explanations for the challenge of discovering a new world.

She looked again at the three naked women lying on the ground, arms outstretched, and tried to clothe them again in the colour of the aura they emanated. They were now travelling through Time and meeting many lost Soulmates. Those three women would, from that night on, plunge into the mission that had been awaiting them since they were born. One was over sixty, but age was of no importance. What mattered was that they were finally face to face with the destiny that had been patiently awaiting them, and from now on they would use their Gifts to keep safe certain crucial plants in God's garden. Each one had arrived at this place for different reasons – a failed love affair, a sense of weariness with routine or perhaps a search for Power. They had confronted fear, inertia and the many disappointments that assail those who follow the path of magic. But the fact is, they had reached the place they needed to reach, for the Hand of God always guides those who follow their path with faith.

'The Tradition of the Moon is a fascinating one, with its Teachers and its rituals, but there is another Tradition too,' thought the Magus, his eyes still fixed on Brida, and feeling slightly envious of Wicca, who would remain by her side for a long time. That other Tradition was a more difficult one to follow because it was simple and simple things always seem so complicated. Its Teachers lived in the world, and did not always realise the importance of what they were teaching, because the impulse behind that teaching often seemed nothing more than an absurd impulse. They were carpenters, poets, mathematicians, people from all professions and walks of life, who lived scattered throughout the world. People who suddenly felt the need to talk to someone, to explain a feeling they couldn't quite understand, but which was impossible to keep to themselves, and that was the way in which the Tradition of the Sun kept its knowledge alive. The impulse of Creation.

Wherever there were people, there was always some trace of the Tradition of the Sun. Sometimes it was a sculpture, sometimes a table, at others a few lines from a poem passed from generation to generation by a particular group or tribe. The people through which the Tradition of the Sun spoke were people just like anyone else, and who, one morning or one evening, looked at the world and felt the presence of something greater. They had unwittingly plunged into an unknown sea, and, for the most part, they did not do so again. Everyone, at least once in each incarnation, possessed the secret of the Universe.

They found themselves momentarily immersed in the Dark Night, but, lacking sufficient self-belief, they rarely returned to it. And the Sacred Heart, which nourished the world with love and peace and devotion found itself once more surrounded by thorns.

Wicca was glad she was a Teacher of the Tradition of the Moon. Everyone who came to her was eager to learn, while, in the Tradition of the Sun, most were in permanent flight from what life was teaching them.

'Not that it matters,' thought Wicca, because the age of miracles was returning, and no one could remain indifferent to the changes the world was beginning to experience. Within a few years, the power of the Tradition of the Sun would reveal itself in all its brilliance. Anyone not already following their own path would begin to feel dissatisfied with themselves and be forced to make a choice: they would either have to accept an existence beset with disappointment and pain or else come to realise that everyone was born to be happy. Having made their choice, they would have no option but to change, and the great struggle, the Jihad, would begin.

With one perfect movement of her hand, Wicca drew a circle in the air with her dagger. Inside that invisible circle, she drew a five-pointed star, which witches call the pentagram. The pentagram was the symbol of the elements at work in mankind, and through it, the women lying on the ground would now come into contact with the world of light.

'Close your eyes,' said Wicca.

The three women obeyed.

Above the head of each of them Wicca performed the ritual moves with her dagger.

'Now open the eyes of your souls.'

rida opened the eyes of her soul. She was in a desert and the place looked very familiar.

She remembered that she had been there before. With the Magus.

She looked around, but couldn't see him. Yet she wasn't afraid; she felt calm and happy. She knew who she was and where she lived; she knew that in some other place in time a party was going on. But none of this mattered, because the landscape before her was so much prettier: the sand, the mountains in the distance and a huge stone.

'Welcome,' said a voice.

Beside her stood a gentleman wearing clothes like those worn by her grandfather.

'I am Wicca's Teacher. When you become a Teacher, your students will find Wicca here, and so on and so forth until the Soul of the World finally makes itself manifest.'

'I'm at a ritual for witches,' Brida said, 'a Sabbath.'

The Teacher laughed.

'You have found your path. Few people have the courage to do so. They prefer to follow a path that is not their own. Everyone has a Gift, but they choose not to see it. You accepted yours, and your encounter with your Gift is your encounter with the world.'

'But why?'

'So that you can plant God's garden.'

'I have a life ahead of me,' said Brida. 'I want to live that life just like anyone else. I want to be able to make mistakes, to be selfish, to have faults.'

The Teacher smiled. In his right hand a blue cloak suddenly appeared.

'You can only be close to people if you are one of them.'

The scene around her changed. She was no longer in a desert, but immersed in a kind of liquid, in which various strange creatures were swimming.

'Life is about making mistakes,' said the Teacher. 'Cells went on reproducing themselves in exactly the same way for millions of years, until one of them made a mistake, and introduced change into that endless cycle of repetition.'

Brida was gazing in amazement at the sea. She didn't ask how it was possible for them to breathe in there; all she could hear was the Teacher's voice, all she could think of was a very similar journey she had made and which had begun in a field of wheat.

'It was a mistake that set the world in motion,' said the Teacher. 'Never be afraid of making a mistake.'

'But Adam and Eve were driven out of Paradise.'

'And they will return one day knowing the miracle of the heavens and of all the world. God knew what he was doing when he drew their attention to the tree of the Knowledge of Good and Evil. If he hadn't wanted them to eat it, he would never have mentioned it.'

'So why did he, then?'

'In order to set the Universe in motion.'

The scene changed back to the desert and the stone. It was morning, and the horizon was becoming suffused with pink light. The Teacher came towards her with the cloak.

'I consecrate you now, in this moment. Your Gift is God's instrument. May you prove to be a useful tool.'

Wicca picked up the dress belonging to the youngest of the three women and held it up in her two hands. She made a symbolic offering to the Celtic priests who, in astral form, were watching everything from above the trees. Then she turned to the young woman.

'Stand up,' she said.

Brida stood up. The shadows from the fire flickered over her naked body. Once, another body had been consumed by those same flames, but that time was over.

'Raise your arms.'

Brida raised her arms. Wicca put the dress on her.

'I was naked,' she said to the Teacher, when he had wrapped the cloak about her. 'And I was not ashamed.'

'If it wasn't for shame, God would never have discovered that Adam and Eve had eaten the apple.'

The Teacher was watching the sunrise. He seemed distracted, but he wasn't. Brida knew this.

'Never be ashamed,' he said. 'Accept what life offers you and try to drink from every cup. All wines should be tasted; some should only be sipped, but with others, drink the whole bottle.'

'How will I know which is which?'

'By the taste. You can only know a good wine if you have first tasted a bad one.'

Wicca turned Brida round to face the fire, then moved on to the next Initiate. The fire picked up the energy of her Gift so that it could be made manifest in her. At that moment, Brida was watching a sunrise, a sun that would, from then on, light the rest of her life.

'Now you must go,' said the Teacher, as soon as the sun had risen.

'I'm not afraid of my Gift,' Brida told him. 'I know where I'm going and what I'm going to do. I know that someone helped me to arrive here.

'I've been here before. There were people dancing and a secret temple built to celebrate the Tradition of the Moon.'

The Teacher said nothing. He turned to her and made a sign with his right hand.

'You have been accepted. May your path be one of peace in times of peace, and of combat in times of combat. Never confuse one with the other.'

* * *

The figure of the Teacher began to dissolve, along with the desert and the stone. Only the sun remained, but the sun began to become one with the sky. Then the sky grew dark, and the sun became more like the flames of a fire.

She was back. She remembered everything now: the noise, the clapping, the dancing, the trance. She remembered having taken off her clothes in front of all these people, and now she felt rather awkward. But she also remembered her meeting with the Teacher. She tried to master her feelings of shame and fear and anxiety – they would always be with her, and she must get used to them.

Wicca asked the three Initiates to stand in the very middle of the semicircle formed by the women. The witches joined hands and made a ring.

They sang songs that no one now dared to accompany; the sounds flowed from their barely open lips, creating a strange vibration, which grew ever shriller, until it resembled the cry of some crazed bird. At some point in the future, she would learn how to make those sounds. She would learn many more things, until she became a Teacher too. Then other men and women would be initiated by her into the Tradition of the Moon.

All of this, however, would happen at the appointed moment. She had all the time in the world, now that she had found her destiny again, and had someone to help her. Eternity was hers.

Everyone appeared to have strange colours around them, and Brida felt slightly bewildered. She liked the world as it had been before.

The witches stopped singing.

'The Initiation of the Moon is finished and complete,' said Wicca. 'The world is now a field, and you will work to make sure that there is a good harvest.'

'I feel strange,' said one of the Initiates. 'Everything's blurred.'

'What you're seeing is the energy field that surrounds each individual, their aura, as we call it. That is the first step along the path of the Great Mysteries. The sensation will soon fade, and later I will teach you how to awaken it again.'

With one swift, agile movement, she flung her ritual dagger to the ground. It stuck fast, the handle still trembling with the force of the impact.

'The ceremony is over,' she said.

rida went over to Lorens. His eyes were shining, and she felt how very proud he was of her and how much he loved her. They could grow together, create a new way of living, discover a whole Universe that lay before them, just waiting for people of courage like them.

But there was another man too. While she was talking to Wicca's Teacher, she had made her choice, because that other man would be able to take her hand during difficult moments, and lead her with experience and love through the Dark Night of Faith. She would learn to love him, and her love for him would be as great as her respect. They were both walking the same road to knowledge, and because of him she had reached the point where she was now. With him, she would one day learn the Tradition of the Sun.

Now she knew that she was a witch. She had learned the art of witchcraft over many centuries and was back where she should be. From that night on, Wisdom and knowledge would be the most important things in her life.

'We can leave now,' she said to Lorens. He was gazing with admiration at this woman dressed all in black; Brida, however, knew that the Magus would be seeing her dressed all in blue.

She held out the bag containing her other clothes.

'You go ahead and see if you can get us a lift. I need to speak to someone.'

Lorens took the bag, but only went a little way towards the path through the forest. The ritual was over and they were back in the world of men, with their loves, their jealousies and their wars of conquest.

Fear had come back too. Brida was behaving oddly.

'I don't know if God exists,' he said to the trees around him. 'And yet I can't think about that now, because I, too, am face to face with the mystery.'

He felt he was talking in a different way, with a strange confidence he had never known he possessed. But, at that moment, he believed that the trees were listening to him.

'The people here may not understand me; they may despise my efforts, but I know that I'm as brave as they are, because I seek God even though I don't believe in him. If he exists, he is the God of the Brave.'

Lorens noticed that his hands were trembling slightly. The night had passed and he had understood nothing of what went on. He knew that he had entered into a trance state, but that was all. However, the fact that his hands were shaking had nothing to do with that plunge into the Dark Night, as Brida called it.

He looked up at the sky, still full of low clouds. God was the God of the Brave. And He would understand him, because the brave are those who make decisions despite their fear, who are tormented by the Devil every step of the way and gripped by anxiety about their every action, wondering if they are right or wrong. And yet, nevertheless, they act. They do so because they also believe in miracles, like the witches who had danced round the fire that night.

God might be trying to return to him through that woman who was now walking away towards another man. If she left, perhaps God would leave forever. She was his opportunity, because she knew that the best way to immerse oneself in God was through love. He didn't want to lose the chance of getting her back.

He took a deep breath, feeling the cold, pure air of the forest in his lungs, and he made a sacred promise to himself.

God was the God of the Brave.

Brida walked over to the Magus. They met by the fire. Words came only with difficulty.

She was the one to break the silence.

'We are on the same path.'

He nodded.

'So let us follow it together.'

'But you don't love me,' said the Magus.

'I do love you. I don't yet know my love for you, but I do love you. You're my Soulmate.'

The Magus still had a distant look in his eye. He was thinking about the Tradition of the Sun, and how one of the most important lessons of the Tradition of the Sun was Love. Love was the only bridge between the visible and the invisible known to everyone. It was the only effective language for translating the lessons that the Universe taught to human beings every day.

'I'm not going anywhere,' she said. 'I'm staying with you.'

'Your boyfriend is waiting,' replied the Magus. 'I will bless your love.'

Brida looked at him, puzzled.

'No one can possess a sunset like the one we saw that evening,' he went on. 'Just as no one can possess an afternoon of rain beating against the window, or the serenity of a sleeping child, or the magical moment when the waves break on the rocks. No one can possess the beautiful things of this Earth, but we can know them and love them. It is through such moments that God reveals himself to mankind.

'We are not the masters of the sun or of the afternoon or of the waves or even of the vision of God, because we cannot possess ourselves.'

The Magus held out his hand to Brida and gave her a flower.

'When we first met – although it seems to me that I've always known you, because I can't remember the world before that – I showed you the Dark Night. I wanted to see how you would face up to your own limitations. I knew that you were my Soulmate, and that you would teach me everything I needed to learn – that is why God divided man and woman.'

Brida touched the flower. It seemed to her that it was the first flower she had seen in months. Spring had arrived.

'People give flowers as presents because flowers contain the true meaning of Love. Anyone who tries to possess a flower will have to watch its beauty fading. But if you simply look at a flower in a field, you will keep it forever, because the flower is part of the evening and the sunset and the smell of damp earth and the clouds on the horizon.'

Brida was looking at the flower. The Magus took it from her and returned it to the forest.

Brida's eyes filled with tears. She was proud of her Soulmate.

'That is what the forest taught me. That you will never be mine, and that is why I will never lose you. You were my hope during my days of loneliness, my anxiety during moments of doubt, my certainty during moments of faith.

'Knowing that my Soulmate would come one day, I devoted myself to learning the Tradition of the Sun. Knowing that you existed was my one reason for continuing to live.'

Brida could no longer conceal her tears.

'Then you came, and I understood all of this. You came to free me from the slavery I myself had created, to tell me that I was free to return to the world and to the things of the world. I understood everything I needed to know, and I love you more than all the women I have ever known, more than I loved the woman who, quite unwittingly, exiled me to the forest. I will always remember now that love is liberty. That was the lesson it took me so many years to learn. That is the lesson that sent me into exile and now sets me free again.'

The flames crackled in the fire, and a few latecomers were beginning to say their goodbyes. But Brida wasn't listening to anything that was going on around her.

'Brida!' she heard a distant voice call.

'Here's looking at you, kid,' said the Magus. It was a line from an old film he had seen once. He felt happy because he had turned another important page in the Tradition of the Sun. He felt the presence of his Teacher, who had chosen that night for his new Initiation.

'I will always remember you, and you will remember me, just as we will remember the evening, the rain on the windows, and all the things we'll always have because we cannot possess them.'

'Brida!' Lorens called again.

'Go in peace,' said the Magus. 'And dry those tears, or tell him that the smoke from the fire got in your eyes. Never forget me.'

He knew he didn't need to say this, but he said it anyway.

Wicca noticed that some people had left a few of their belongings behind. She would have to phone them and tell them to come and fetch them.

'The fire will have burned down soon,' she said.

He remained silent. There were still a few flames, and he still had his eyes fixed on them.

'I don't regret that I once fell in love with you,' Wicca went on.

'Nor do I,' replied the Magus.

She felt an enormous desire to talk about Brida, but she said nothing. The eyes of the man beside her inspired respect and wisdom.

'It's a shame I'm not your Soulmate,' she added. 'We would have made a good couple.'

But the Magus wasn't listening to what Wicca was saying. There was a vast world before him and many things to do. He had to help plant God's garden, he had to teach people to teach themselves. He would meet other women, fall in love, and live this incarnation as intensely as he could. That night completed one stage of his existence, and a new Dark Night lay ahead, but the next stage would be much more enjoyable and joyful, much closer to what he had dreamed. He knew this because of the flowers and the forests and because of young women who arrive one day led by God's hand, not knowing that they are there in order for destiny to be fulfilled. He knew this because of the Tradition of the Moon and the Tradition of the Sun.

Author Biography: Paulo Coelho

Paulo Coelho was born in Rio in August 1947, the son of Pedro Queima Coelho de Souza, an engineer, and his wife Lygia, a homemaker. Early on, Coelho dreamed of an artistic career, something frowned upon in his middle-class household. In the austere surroundings of a strict Jesuit school, Coelho discovered his true vocation: to be a writer. Coelho's parents, however, had different plans for him. When their attempts to suppress his devotion to literature failed, they took it as a sign of mental illness. When Coelho was seventeen, his father twice had him committed to a mental institution, where he endured sessions of electroconvulsive 'therapy'. His parents brought him back to the institution once more, after he became involved with a theatre group and started to work as a journalist.

Coelho was always a nonconformist and a seeker of the new. When, in the excitement of 1968, the guerrilla and hippy movements took hold in a Brazil ruled by a repressive military regime, Coelho embraced progressive politics and joined the peace and love generation. He sought spiritual experiences travelling all over Latin America in the footsteps of Carlos Castaneda. He worked in the theatre and dabbled in journalism, launching an alternative magazine called *2001*. He began to collaborate with music producer Raul Seixas as a lyricist, transforming the Brazilian rock scene. In 1973 Coelho and Raul joined the Alternative Society, an organisation that defended the individual's right to free expression, and began publishing a series of comic strips, calling for more freedom. Members of the organisation were detained and imprisoned. Two days later, Coelho was kidnapped and tortured by a group of paramilitaries.

This experience affected him profoundly. At the age of twenty-six, Coelho decided that he had had enough of living on the edge and wanted to be 'normal'. He worked as an executive in the music industry. He tried his hand at writing but didn't start seriously until after he had an encounter with a stranger. The man first came to him in a vision, and two months later Coelho met him at a café in Amsterdam. The stranger suggested that Coelho should return to Catholicism and study the benign side of magic. He also encouraged Coelho to walk the Road to Santiago, the medieval pilgrims' route.

In 1987 a year after completing that pilgrimage, Coelho wrote *The Pilgrimage*. The book describes his experiences and his discovery that the extraordinary occurs in the lives of ordinary people. A year later, Coelho wrote a very different book, *The Alchemist*. The first edition sold only nine hundred copies and the publishing house decided not to reprint it.

Coelho would not surrender his dream. He found another publishing house, a bigger one. He wrote *Brida*; the book received a lot of attention in the press, and both *The Alchemist* and *The Pilgrimage* appeared on bestseller lists.

Paulo has gone on to write many other bestselling books, including *The Valkyries, By the River Piedra I Sat Down and Wept, The Fifth Mountain, Manual of the Warrior of Light, Veronika Decides to Die, Eleven Minutes, The Zahir, The Devil and Miss Prym* and *Like the Flowing River*.

Today, Paulo Coelho's books appear at the top of bestseller lists worldwide. In 2002 the *Jornal de Letras de Portugal*, the foremost literary authority in the Portuguese language, bestowed upon *The Alchemist* the title of most sold book in the history of the language. In 2003 Coelho's novel *Eleven Minutes* was the world's bestselling fiction title (*USA Today, Publishing Trends*).

In addition to his novels, Coelho writes a globally syndicated weekly newspaper column and occasionally publishes articles on current affairs. His newsletter, *The Manual On-Line*, has over 70,000 subscribers.

Coelho and his wife, Christina Oiticica, are the founders of the Paulo Coelho Institute, which provides support and opportunities for underprivileged mem-bers of Brazilian society.

Life is a
journey

Make sure you don't miss a thing.
Live it with Paulo Coelho.

What are you searching for?

A transforming journey on the pilgrims' road to Santiago - and the first of Paulo's extraordinary books.

The Pilgrimage

Do you believe in yourself?

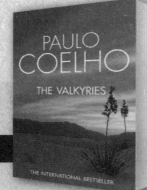

A modern-day adventure in the searing heat of the Mojave desert and an exploration of fear and self-doubt.

The Valkyries

How do we see the amazing in every day?

When two young lovers are reunited, they discover anew the truth of what lies in their hearts.

By the River Piedra, I Sat Down and Wept

Is life always worth living?

A fundamental moral question explored as only Paulo Coelho can.

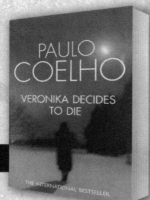

Veronika Decides to Die

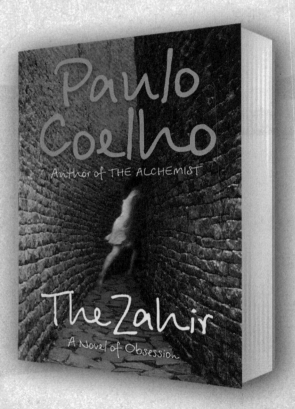

Could you be tempted into evil?

The inhabitants of a small town are challenged by a mysterious stranger to choose between good and evil.

The Devil and Miss Prym

Can faith triumph over suffering?

Paulo Coelho's brilliant telling of the story of Elijah, who was forced to choose between love and duty.

The Fifth Mountain

Can sex be sacred?

An unflinching exploration of the lengths we go to in our search for love, sex and spirituality.

Eleven Minutes

Are you brave enough to live your dream?

Strategies and inspiration to help you follow your own path in a troubled world.

Manual of the Warrior of Light

What does it mean to be truly alive?

An intimate collection of reflections and short stories about living and dying, destiny and choice, love lost and found.

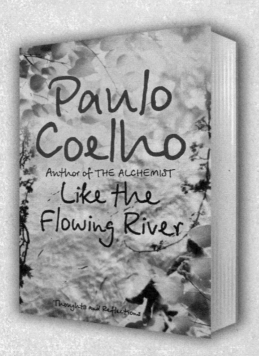

How do we find the courage to always be true to ourselves?

Who is the Witch of Portobello? Discover her life through a series of interviews with those who knew her ... told with Coelho's inimitable philosophical style.

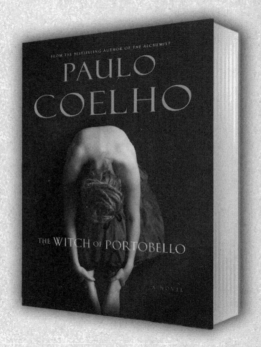

How will I know who my Soulmate is?

The story of Brida and her quest for knowledge.

Feeling
inspired?

Discover more about the
world of Paulo Coelho.